"You Daltons always expect to get your way." Amelia's tone was resentful, and she didn't care.

"Not always." Seth smiled sardonically. "But we usually do." He took both her hands in his. His palms had the calluses of a workingman on them.

She smiled with nostalgic sadness remembering the sixteen-year-old girl she'd once been. The one with the crush on Seth.

"What are you thinking?" Seth asked quietly. To her surprise, he cupped her face and gazed into her eyes for a few seconds before leaning closer and touching her lips with his. The kiss was the gentlest she'd ever known and caused a rain of tears inside her.

When he lifted his head, he said enigmatically, "I'm not the person you think I am."

With that, he was gone.

She touched her lips as if she could feel the imprint of his kiss there. "Then who are you?" she murmured.

Dear Reader,

We're delighted to feature Jennifer Mikels, who penned the second story in our multiple-baby-focused series, MANHATTAN MULTIPLES. Jennifer writes, "To me, there's something wonderfully romantic about a doctor-nurse story and about a crush developing into a forever love. In *The Fertility Factor* (#1559), a woman's love touches a man's heart and teaches him that what he thought was impossible is within his reach if he'll trust her enough."

Sherryl Woods continues to captivate us with *Daniel's Desire* (#1555), the conclusion of her celebrated miniseries THE DEVANEYS. When a runaway girl crosses their paths, a hero and heroine reunite despite their tragic past. And don't miss *Prince and Future...Dad?* (#1556), the second book in Christine Rimmer's exciting miniseries VIKING BRIDES, in which a princess experiences a night of passion and gets the surprise of a lifetime! *Quinn's Woman* (#1557), by Susan Mallery is the next in her longtime-favorite HOMETOWN HEARTBREAKERS miniseries. Here, a self-defense expert never expects to find hand-to-heart combat with her rugged instructor....

Return to the latest branch of popular miniseries MONTANA MAVERICKS: THE KINGSLEYS with *Marry Me...Again* (#1558) by Cheryl St.John. This dramatic tale shows a married couple experiencing some emotional bumps—namely that their marriage is invalid! Will they break all ties or rediscover a love that's always been there? Then, *Found in Lost Valley* (#1560) by Laurie Paige, the fourth title in her SEVEN DEVILS miniseries, is about two people with secrets in their pasts, but who can't deny the rising tensions between them!

As you can see, we have a lively batch of stories, delivering diversity and emotion in each romance.

Happy reading!

Sincerely,

Karen Taylor Richman
Senior Editor

Please address questions and book requests to:
Silhouette Reader Service
U.S.: 3010 Walden Ave., P.O. Box 1325, Buffalo, NY 14269
Canadian: P.O. Box 609, Fort Erie, Ont. L2A 5X3

Found in Lost Valley

LAURIE PAIGE

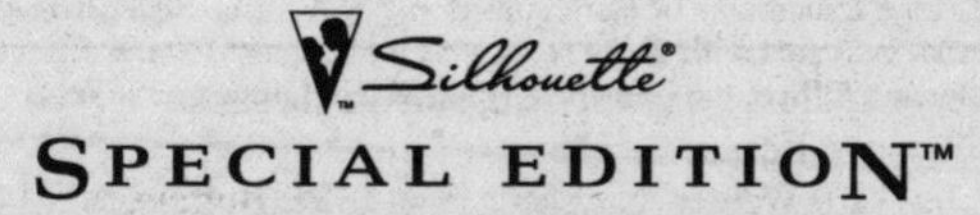

Published by Silhouette Books
America's Publisher of Contemporary Romance

To our own Galadriel:
May fantasy light your path forever....

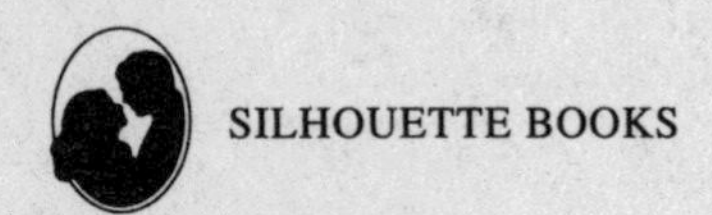

ISBN 0-373-24560-2

FOUND IN LOST VALLEY

This edition published by arrangement with Harlequin Books S.A.

Visit Silhouette at www.eHarlequin.com

Printed in U.S.A.

Books by Laurie Paige

Silhouette Special Edition

Lover's Choice #170
Man Without a Past #755
**Home for a Wild Heart* #828
**A Place for Eagles* #839
**The Way of a Man* #849
**Wild Is the Wind* #887
**A River To Cross* #910
Molly Darling #1021
Live-In Mom #1077
The Ready-Made Family #1114
Husband: Bought and Paid For #1139
A Hero's Homecoming #1178
Warrior's Woman #1193
Father-To-Be #1201
A Family Homecoming #1292
Make Way for Babies! #1317
***Something To Talk About* #1396
***When I See Your Face* #1408
***When I Dream of You* #1419
The Princess Is Pregnant #1459
Her Montana Man #1483
†*Showdown!* #1532
†*The One and Only* #1545
†*Found in Lost Valley* #1560

Silhouette Desire

Gypsy Enchantment #123
Journey to Desire #195
Misty Splendor #304
Golden Promise #404

Silhouette Yours Truly

Christmas Kisses for a Dollar
Only One Groom Allowed

Harlequin Duets
The Cowboy Next Door

Silhouette Romance

South of the Sun #296
A Tangle of Rainbows #333
A Season for Butterflies #364
Nothing Lost #382
The Sea at Dawn #398
A Season for Homecoming #727
Home Fires Burning Bright #733
Man from the North Country #772
‡*Cara's Beloved* #917
‡*Sally's Beau* #923
‡*Victoria's Conquest* #933
Caleb's Son #994
**A Rogue's Heart* #1013
An Unexpected Delivery #1151
Wanted: One Son #1246
The Guardian's Bride #1318

Silhouette Books

Montana Mavericks
The Once and Future Wife
Father Found

The Fortunes of Texas
The Baby Pursuit

The Coltons
The Housekeeper's Daughter

Lone Star Country Club
Heartbreaker

Under Western Skies
"One Baby To Go Please"

Montana Mavericks:
Wed in Whitehorn
Cheyenne Bride
Outlaw Marriage

Claiming His Own collection
†*Something to Hide*

*Wild River
**The Windraven Legacy
‡All-American Sweethearts
†Seven Devils

LAURIE PAIGE

Along with her writing adventures, Laurie has been a NASA engineer, a past president of the Romance Writers of America, a mother and a grandmother. She was twice a Romance Writers of America RITA® Award finalist for Best Traditional Romance and has won awards from *Romantic Times* for Best Silhouette Special Edition and Best Silhouette. She has resettled in Northern California.

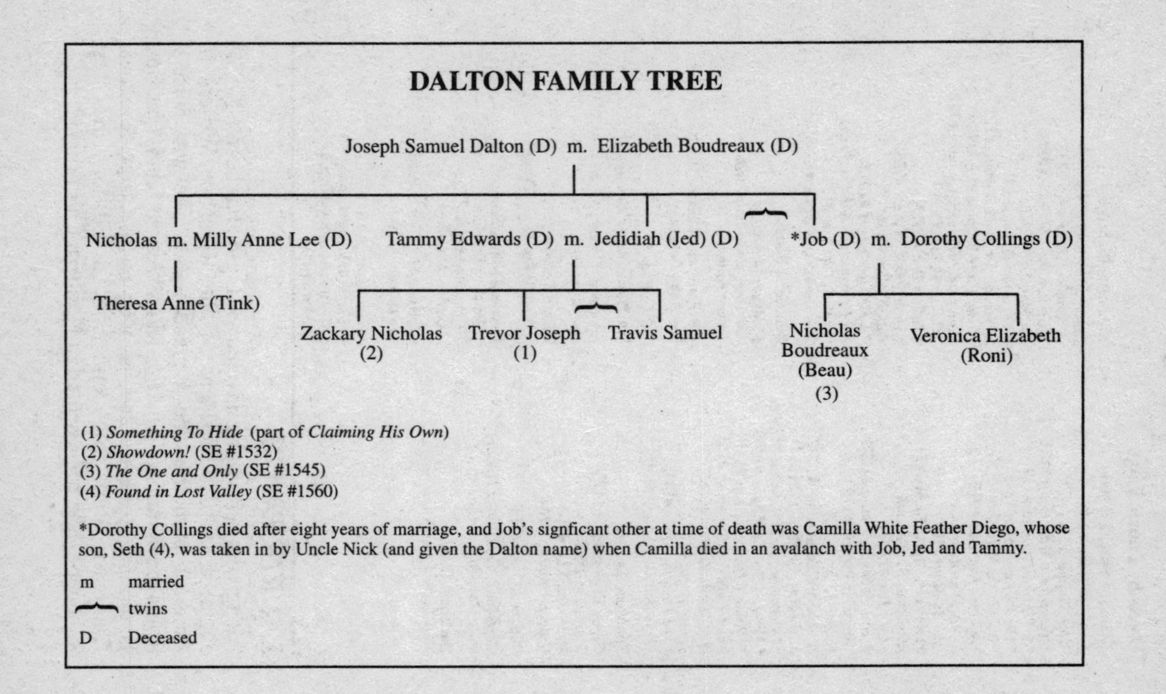
DALTON FAMILY TREE
Joseph Samuel Dalton (D) m. Elizabeth Boudreaux (D)
Nicholas m. Milly Anne Lee (D)
Tammy Edwards (D) m. Jedidiah (Jed) (D)
*Job (D) m. Dorothy Collings (D)
Theresa Anne (Tink)
Zackary Nicholas (2)
Trevor Joseph (1)
Travis Samuel
Nicholas Boudreaux (Beau) (3)
Veronica Elizabeth (Roni)
(1) Something To Hide (part of Claiming His Own)
(2) Showdown! (SE #1532)
(3) The One and Only (SE #1545)
(4) Found in Lost Valley (SE #1560)
*Dorothy Collings died after eight years of marriage, and Job's signficant other at time of death was Camilla White Feather Diego, whose son, Seth (4), was taken in by Uncle Nick (and given the Dalton name) when Camilla died in an avalanch with Job, Jed and Tammy.
m married
twins
D Deceased

Chapter One

Amelia Miller glanced up when the wind rattled the windowpanes of the Victorian house. The old mansion had withstood fiercer storms than this one in its hundred and twenty years. Although, she admitted, this first rain of October was not a gentle one.

She stuck her toes closer to the glowing gas-log fireplace. The temperature was thirty-eight degrees outside, the rooms of the bed-and-breakfast were filled for the weekend and the guests were snug inside, the last one arriving little more than an hour ago.

All was well in her little corner of the world.

Most of her clients were couples who'd come up

from Boise for a weekend of hiking. The colors of autumn covered the hills, and the aspens and cottonwoods were especially beautiful this year. She hoped the rain didn't spoil the outing for the nature lovers.

Glancing at the clock, she saw it was nearly eleven o'clock. She yawned, finished off the herbal tea and closed the novel she'd been reading. The historical romance story was about knights and ladies and honor, which the hero had in abundance, perhaps to the point of obstinacy.

There were worse faults, she mused. For a moment, she remembered being twenty and swept off her feet by a handsome cowboy in town for the rodeo trials. After knowing him all of two weeks, she'd married him and taken off on an exciting adventure.

The excitement had lasted about two months, the marriage nearly two years, mostly due to her own stubbornness in refusing to give up. Her dashing cowboy had a temper and a mean streak. When she'd urged him to go to anger management counseling, he'd hit her. She'd packed and left, finally admitting she'd made a serious mistake.

At thirty-three, she had few illusions about life. Now, happiness was a full house and a roof that didn't leak. So much for young love and the dreams that went with it.

She smiled at her long-ago idealism, somewhat saddened by the loss, then yawned again. Time for bed. Five-thirty came early—

The *br-r-ring* of the doorbell startled her. Slipping on fuzzy scuffs, she went silently down the hall into the main room, making sure her robe was securely closed as she did.

Then she peered out through one of the etched glass panels of the door.

The carriage lamps on each side illuminated a lone man standing there, his head tilted down as if he was deep in thought, his hands in the pockets of a trench coat that glistened with rain across the broad shoulders.

"Yes?" she said without opening the door.

"Amelia? It's Seth Dalton."

At sixteen, her heart had nearly leaped out of her body each time she'd encountered the oldest of the six Dalton orphans. At present, she was only mildly surprised. One or another of the Dalton clan was often at her place. She unlocked the door and stood aside.

"What a terrible night to be out," she said when he entered the lobby, after carefully removing the raincoat and shaking off the water droplets on the porch.

He closed the door, dropped a duffel bag at his feet and hung the coat on a hook. "Yeah, terrible," he agreed, with a smile that was definitely weary.

"Uh, was I expecting you?"

"No. I was heading for the ranch but got out of the city later than I'd planned. With the rain and the Friday night traffic, there was a big wreck. I sat on the freeway for nearly three hours. Since it's so late, I decided to stop here.''

She made sympathetic noises.

''I hope you have a room. I'm beat,'' he continued.

''Well, actually, we're full this weekend. People come up for the turning of the leaves,'' she explained, when he gave her a surprised glance tinged with a bit of annoyance, from those dark eyes so at odds with the usual Dalton sky-blue, to-die-for color.

''What about the single room?''

''It's taken, too. A lone hiker showed up earlier this evening. About an hour ago,'' she added as a frown formed a line between those thick, black masculine eyebrows.

Seth heaved a sigh and nodded. ''I guess I'll go on to the ranch then.''

Nicholas Dalton, who had taken in the orphans when his two younger brothers were killed in a freak avalanche some twenty-two or so years ago, lived on the original Dalton homestead, which was thirty miles from the tiny town of Lost Valley.

On country roads that wound into the Seven Devils Mountains of Idaho, the trip would take an hour in the pouring rain. If the road was washed out somewhere along the way, it might be impassible. Seth would be stranded for the second time that night.

In the rain. In the mountains. In the chilling cold.

Amelia glanced at the furniture in the great room,

consisting mostly of tables and chairs, with a Victorian sofa and divan for period ambiance in front of the fireplace, and made a decision. ''There's a sofa bed in my sitting room. You can sleep there if you like.''

''I would,'' he at once agreed.

His grin flashed in the dim light, his teeth brilliant in contrast to his dark hair and swarthy skin tones. Seth's mother had been Latino or Native American—Amelia wasn't sure which—and he'd inherited his dark good looks from her.

An inch under six feet, he was a bit shorter than his male cousins, but his build was the most muscular. In his senior year in high school, he'd played quarterback in football, and, with the strength in those broad shoulders, he'd become known for long, accurate passes that often saved the game for the home team. All the girls had had terrible crushes on him, including Amelia.

''Lead the way,'' he suggested, picking up the duffel bag and giving her an expectant glance.

Rebounding to the present, she locked the door and led him along the hall to the back of the house and into her quarters, which consisted of a sitting room looking out on the garden, a bedroom and a bath. She'd converted the butler's pantry into a walk-in closet, so there was ample privacy for her and space for her personal belongings.

''Would you like to take a warm shower?'' she asked. ''Or dry your hair? There's a blow dryer in the bath.''

"That would be great."

"Through here," she said, going into her bedroom and pointing out the bathroom door. "Towels are in the basket beside the tub."

While he disappeared into the other room, she quickly collected sheets, blankets and a pillow, took them to the sitting room and made up the bed for him after unfolding the mattress part of the short sofa.

She wondered if she should offer him her bed, since it was queen-size and the sofa wasn't. But then, she would have to get to the bathroom and her clothing in the bedroom closet and would probably wake him in the morning, while from her bedroom she could quietly dress and sneak out through the sitting room without disturbing his sleep.

The shower stopped, and the whine of the hair dryer came on a minute later.

Amelia crossed the hall to the kitchen. There, she made a cup of hot cocoa, then prepared one for herself just to be companionable. She warmed muffins in the microwave and returned to the sitting room, tray in hand.

"That smells delicious," Seth told her.

He stood in the doorway to the bedroom, dressed in gray sweatpants but no shirt. Dark hair formed an enticing pillow on his chest. He placed his shoes and duffel beside the bed. His long, narrow feet were clad in thick socks. Her heart fluttered a bit as it had when she was a girl.

''Banana-nut muffins. I thought you might be hungry after the long trip,'' she said.

''I wasn't, but I am now.''

His voice seemed deeper, somehow darker and more mysterious suddenly. She wondered if she imagined it. She set the tray on the coffee table and took a seat in her favorite chintz-covered rocker near one corner of the brick hearth. Drawing a deep breath, she picked up a mug and invited him to help himself.

He pulled on a sweatshirt, then sat in the chenille easy chair and propped his feet on the bricks close to the fire. Behind them, the sofa bed beckoned the weary to stretch out and relax. The clock on the mantel ticked in its friendly fashion.

Amelia became aware of the lateness of the hour and the intimacy of the setting as a fresh assault of wind and rain hit the windows.

''Not a fit night for man or beast,'' Seth said, peering out at the wet landscape lit by carriage lamps and tiny spotlights along the paths and among the foliage.

''True,'' she said, sipping her cocoa since she couldn't think of anything else to say.

His laughter caused her hand to jerk. The hot liquid splashed over the rim of the cup. She quickly licked it away before it could drip on her robe.

''Sorry,'' he said softly, amusement still in his eyes.

''That's okay.'' She wondered what he found funny. Since he'd been looking at her, and continued to do so, she self-consciously wiped her mouth and chin. Her fingers trembled ever so slightly.

"Relax," he murmured. "I know we Dalton boys have questionable reputations, but Uncle Nick doesn't allow us to pounce on women, especially those who come to our aid and give us refuge during storms."

For a second of insanity, Amelia wished he would do just that, then was appalled at herself. The Daltons were a prominent family in this part of Idaho. Other than during one long-ago incident, Seth had never displayed any attraction to her—a vagabond child who'd been shipped to Lost Valley to stay with her grandparents each time her parents had quarreled and split up. She'd spent most of her high school years here, but in two- to six-month stretches as the marriage waxed and waned.

The despair and resignation of that child rose in her, reminding her that, other than her grandparents, she'd never been able to depend on anyone in her life….

She stopped the morbid thoughts and wondered what had brought such gloom to her spirits. The storm, she decided, observing the torrents of rain against the window. Summoning a smile, she murmured in a teasing tone, "It would never occur to me that you would act less than a gentleman."

The dark eyebrows rose. "Don't be too sure of that," he warned, a thread of humor in his voice, but something more, too—an edginess that had nothing to do with the long trip and fatigue, but everything to do with being a man alone with a woman at a late hour, with a bed tantalizingly close.

His eyes swept over her, pausing at the ridiculous pink fuzzy scuffs that had been a gift from her mother last Christmas. Her mom liked frivolous things and thought Amelia was much too staid.

Thinking of her mother's cute, flirty ways that so intrigued men and drove her dad crazy with jealousy, Amelia wished she could think of a sassy comeback. Unfortunately, she never could until long after the opportunity had passed.

Her face warmed, and she hoped the blush wasn't noticeable. With her red hair and fair skin inherited from her grandmother, Amelia found her emotions seemed to lie too close to the surface for her personal comfort.

The wind caused the flames to dance wildly in the grate. She realized she felt the same way inside—sort of wild, as if her spirit wanted to dance, and hot, as if a fire burned in a secret furnace inside her.

"Wasn't that once a wood fireplace?" he asked. "I cleaned the chimneys here one year when your grandparents were still alive."

"I—" She had to clear the huskiness from her throat. "I had it converted to gas this summer. It was too much work to take care of the wood and ashes, but I do enjoy a fire on cold evenings like this."

He nodded in understanding, his eyes half-closed as he gazed at the natural-looking, flaming logs. He had heavy eyelids—bedroom eyes, the girls at school had called them—and the shifting light gave him the dangerous look of a rogue or pirate.

His jawline was strong, his cheeks rather prominent, with interesting shadows beneath them. His lips were evenly matched and his smile entrancing. His hair was curly, which he tried to disguise by keeping it cut short. In school, it had flowed in ripples to his shoulders. She'd wanted to run her fingers through the shining strands.

The telltale heat climbed her neck. Fortunately, he was still gazing into the fire. She found herself staring when he raised the mug to his lips. His throat moved as he swallowed, then he held the mug in both hands, his fingers caressing the smooth porcelain idly, his thoughts faraway as he absently observed the flames.

Her skin tingled all over as if he was stroking her body the way he did the cup. Hunger and longing and a mixture of feelings exploded in her, urgent and reckless. Shocked, she leaped to her feet. "Good night," she said.

He glanced up, surprised at her abrupt action. But Amelia fled to the bedroom and closed the door. She hesitated about locking it, then realized that was silly. He would hardly come charging in after her.

"Good night," she heard him call. "Sweet dreams."

Dreams, she scoffed silently as she climbed into bed a few minutes later. She'd had enough of dreams to last her a lifetime. She was owner of a thriving bed-and-breakfast business, one that she'd built with her own hard work and planning. Who needed dreams?

Everyone, the wind whispered against the dark window, its piping notes somehow sad and more than a little lonely.

Another night flooded her memory, haunting her with the sweet nostalgia of times past, of being sixteen and so very much in love.

Seth turned off the gas to the fake logs in the fireplace and snuggled into bed. The sofa mattress was surprisingly comfortable. He bunched the pillow behind his head, his mind on the woman who slept in the next room.

His libido had acted up while he used her shower. The bathroom was filled with pleasant, feminine scents from shampoo, powder and cologne. Other facets of her personal space also tweaked his imagination, such as the scented candles dotting the wide border of the tub.

The fact that the candles had been used conjured up several intimate scenes. He could picture her relaxing in the tub, that tangled mass of auburn curls pinned up on her head, the candle glow highlighting her fair skin, which looked as delicate as peach petals.

A shudder ran through him and heat erupted deep within. He sucked in air like a man who'd been in danger of smothering. His libido paid no attention to the calming effect this was supposed to produce.

The sheet tented as his body responded in blatant hunger.

Good thing his hostess couldn't see him now. Uncle Nick or no Uncle Nick, Seth would be tempted to forget honor and all that stuff in favor of caveman tactics.

He laughed silently, mockingly. The devil had nothing on his uncle when it came to fury. Uncle Nick was a stickler for proper behavior around the female sex.

Seth agreed with that sentiment. He would never hurt a woman, not intentionally. But there had been one time when he'd been tempted to take all a girl offered.

Amelia at sixteen had been almost more than his seventeen-year-old will could withstand. He could see her now as clearly as he had that night....

Seth had found her standing in the shadows outside the community center, where the Harvest Moon dance was in progress. Even in the dark, he recognized her at once.

''Amelia? What are you doing out here? You'll freeze.'' Like the hero of a novel, he took off his jacket and draped it around her shoulders. The cool night air felt good to him. The dance floor was crowded and all those gyrating bodies caused the temperature to rise.

''Thank you,'' she murmured, ''but I'm okay. Really.'' She returned his jacket.

The fast number ended and a slow love song began. On an impulse, he held out his hands. ''Dance?''

She shook her head and moved more into the shadows.

The rejection intrigued rather than repelled him. ''Come on. We'd better go inside before one of the chaperons finds us and sends us to the principal for skulking in the bushes.''

The attempt at humor failed.

''No, thanks,'' she said. ''I think I'll go home.''

With that, she turned and started across the school parking lot, with only a thin shawl around her shoulders. He tried to recall where she lived. Oh, yes, on the other side of town in a two-story white house with her grandparents.

He'd been on a student council committee with her last year and had delivered some papers to her home. She'd disappeared in March, apparently leaving the area, but had returned a couple of weeks after the start of the new school year. At sixteen, she was nearly a year younger than he was, and a year behind him in school. Like him, she was a member of the Honor Society.

Smart. He liked that in a girl. Last year, as an honor society project, he and Amelia had researched and presented a report on poor scholastic achievement to the school authorities. He'd found her compassionate and thoughtful as well as intelligent. There was also a mystery surrounding her. She appeared and disappeared frequently from the town. When he'd tried to get to know her better, she'd become cool and distant, her manner warning him not to encroach on her privacy. Even so, there was something fragile and beguiling about her, something that had always intrigued him.

He trotted across the pavement and caught up with her. "Your dress is a knockout," he said. "I heard Jennifer Rinquest say she'd kill for it."

"It's my grandmother's," Amelia replied in her usual serious manner. "The taffeta is woven with two different colors so that when the light hits it one way, it looks bronze, but from another angle, it's violet."

"Neat idea."

"Yes."

They were out of the parking lot and on Main Street now. At nearly midnight, there wasn't a car or person to be seen. The shadows were deep between the streetlights, then deeper when Seth and Amelia turned onto the side street where her grandparents lived.

He wondered at her silence. Most girls tended to chatter, he'd found. He didn't feel unwelcome around Amelia, but she didn't try to engage his attention. She had a mysterious aura about her, as if she existed in a time and place that only she could see.

When the light breeze brought her scent to him, his body stirred with a hunger that startled him. Not that that was unusual—Uncle Nick had explained all about hormones and how it was with guys, but different for girls. However, this girl didn't do anything to cause it...other than just be herself. A thought occurred to him. Perhaps the reason she hadn't danced was simply that she didn't know how.

"Uh, would you like me to teach you to dance?"

"No, thanks. I've had lessons," she said in that soft tone that told him nothing. And she turned onto the sidewalk leading to the two-story Victorian.

He stayed with her. "You got a broken leg or something?"

She nimbly climbed the front steps, then turned with a frown. "No."

He grinned. "Sorry. I just wondered why I didn't see you on the floor at the dance."

"No one asked."

Her blunt honesty left him with nothing to say. When she sat in the old-fashioned swing hanging from hooks in a rafter, he joined her. "You didn't have a date?"

She hesitated. "My grandmother arranged for a boy down the street to take me. He disappeared as soon as we got inside the gym." She shrugged. "I didn't mind. It was interesting to watch for a while. Then I decided it was time to come home."

She must have stayed almost four hours, he realized. Long enough that her grandparents wouldn't question why she'd come home early. He propped an arm behind her on the swing. His fingers touched the smooth skin of her shoulder, only partially covered by the cap sleeves of the dress. She was cold. He dropped his arm around her and pulled her close.

"You'll catch a chill," he scolded, sounding very much like his protective uncle.

"I never get sick."

This was said with such world-weary resignation, he was intrigued all over again. What was it with her?

She looped her arms across her middle as if holding inside all that she was so he wouldn't see. He touched her cheek, lingered to stroke the softness there, then tilted her face up to his. Then he kissed her.

The kiss was amazing, shocking, alarming, dazzling, as if stars were falling around them....

The very air went from October cool to July hot in an instant. The warmth of the stars, he thought hazily.

She didn't caress him or even uncross her arms, but her lips...Lord, but those lips were pure liquid fire under his, hesitant at first, then moving, returning the pressure, opening to allow their tongues to meet. It was a kiss unlike any he'd ever experienced, and he'd kissed a lot since becoming cocaptain of the football team last year.

When he lifted his head and gazed down into her face, his heart thudded even harder. In the moonlight, her skin was the pure white of the marble veins he found running through the granite in the mountains. There was something so remote and unexpected about her....

He kissed her again, then groaned and pulled her closer so that they were half lying in the swing, her softness on top, pressing into him. For the first time, he knew, really knew, why kisses weren't enough.

Her breasts were firm against his chest, her lips like cool fire dancing under his. Shifting, he pushed a cushion behind his back and lifted her so that he could slide one leg between hers. Half turning, he captured her body between his and the swing, the movement setting up a brief, wild gyration that broke the kiss.

They clung to each other and, as their eyes met, smiled. For a second, he couldn't breathe, then they were kissing again...and touching in ways he'd never let happen with other girls.

When the need became unbearable, he pulled back enough to ask, ''Where can we go?''

''There's a carriage house,'' she murmured, pressing kisses onto his chest.

He didn't know when or how his shirt became unfastened. The cold air rushing across him brought back a measure of sanity. He held her face between his trembling hands and looked into her eyes.

Hot golden arcs of passionate intensity were visible in those moon-dark depths, along with a sweet vulnerability that reached to his soul. He realized how dangerously, desperately close to the edge they were.

''I have plans,'' he said, summoning the only defense he could think of. ''College. And law school. It'll be years.''

Her expression changed in the blink of an eye, the raw honesty of passion was gone. Sense and caution returned. He felt the loss like the sharp pain of a paper cut.

She sat up and, with quick, precise movements, fitted the bodice of the old-fashioned dress into place, covering the delectable flesh he'd kissed and explored so thoroughly.

"I know," she said in a flat tone that gave nothing away. "It doesn't matter. Thanks for seeing me home."

With that she was gone. He heard the click as the door locked behind her, observed her outline through the etched glass panes as she turned away. That was the last he saw of her until spring. At that time, she returned to school and finished the year, a straight-A student who looked at him with cool blue eyes that didn't invite friendship or confidences anymore.

After graduation he left town on a construction job, then entered the university that fall. He rarely was back for more than a week at a time after that.

Rolling now to one side, then the other, his body tense with the haunting hunger from tonight and the dance long ago, Seth knew he was in for a restless night. Memories and the knowledge that Amelia was only steps away would see to that.

From that intriguing here-today-gone-tomorrow girl, she'd grown into a lovely woman, her gaze still cool, her hair a halo of curls surrounding a heart-shaped face just the way it had that enchanted evening so long ago.

For the oddest moment, he was filled with regret

that they hadn't shared everything the night of the Harvest Moon ball, when their passion had been innocent and honest and so very sweet in a way he couldn't describe. But it was better that they hadn't. Both of them had had a long way to go before they could think seriously of involvement.

So. He'd become an attorney as planned. She'd married, divorced, then returned to Lost Valley and started a very successful bed-and-breakfast inn after her grandparents had passed away within months of each other seven years ago. He'd handled the settling of the estate.

Amelia had changed quite a bit in the intervening years, becoming friendly and outgoing. She'd even played her guitar and sung in a community musical that summer. The appealing vulnerability of youth had disappeared, replaced by the confidence of a woman who knew exactly who she was and where she was going.

Seth wondered what other changes life had made in her, and fell asleep still wondering....

Chapter Two

Amelia opened the door as quietly as possible. It was six o'clock, her usual time to start the workday.

The sitting room was silent and dim in the predawn hour. Treading carefully, she made sure her loafers didn't make a sound on the carpet as she crept by the sofa bed.

Seth lay with one bare arm across his face, the other to the side. The sheet and blanket were pushed halfway down his chest, which was also bare. His long-sleeved shirt lay over the back of the sofa. One leg was outside the covers, the sweatpants apparently providing enough warmth for him.

When he stirred restlessly and kicked the blanket aside, she noticed the definitive ridge on his lower body, clearly outlined by the gray sweats.

A thrill of…shock? surprise? excitement? raced through her entire body with the speed of light. She stood there staring as if she'd never seen a man's aroused body in her life.

Certainly not this man's, some cynical part of her observed, although once they'd kissed and caressed each other with the greatest intimacy she'd ever known. But that was long ago. She'd avoided him after that, just as he had her, his manner pleasant but remote the few times they'd met.

Pulling her gaze from his sleeping form, she hastily stepped forward before her thoughts went even further off track, as her dreams had done last night. Her foot landed on something unexpected, an object that flipped to the side, causing her ankle to turn with a sharp pain.

She flailed her arms, but it was too late; Amelia landed with a muffled grunt right on top of her guest.

With a muttered curse, he sprang instantly awake and into action. Before she could say a word, she was caught in bands of steel, tossed onto her back and held captive against the mattress by hands on her wrists and a long, powerful, masculine body pinning her in place.

She stared at him as if he were indeed a predator about to rip her to shreds. "I'm really sorry," she said in a strangled voice. "I tripped."

His chest moved against her as he inhaled deeply. The ridge she'd noticed was now pressed into her abdomen. It took only a split second for the fact to register; and her eyes flew to his.

He observed her with a harsh, unblinking stare, then slowly relaxed—though not in the lower extremities—and finally he smiled slightly. "You're up early."

"I always get up at five-thirty." Her voice was stilted and defensive. "Please," she added, and moved slightly.

He rolled off her and rose in one smooth motion. She scrambled to a sitting position, pulling her sweater into place over her slacks, then stood, careful to set her feet on the carpet rather than his classy wing-tipped shoes, which, she now realized, were what had tripped her up.

A fierce pain shot up her leg and she sat down abruptly in surprise at this additional indignity. This was *not* going to be her day.

"What is it?" he asked, kicking the shoes aside and settling on his haunches in front of her. "Did you hurt yourself?"

"My ankle, I think." She thought of all the work that had to be done that morning.

"Let me see."

She froze when he lifted her foot, removed her loafer and probed gently. His fingers were long and lean, the skin deeply tanned in contrast to her paleness. Heat swept up her leg to lodge in some turbulent place inside her.

"I'm fine—ouch!" she said.

"There's swelling and bruising already starting

along each side of the ankle bone,'' he told her, examining the place again. ''We need to ice it down before it gets worse.''

''Oh, no, that's okay. I don't have time. I have to help Marta in the kitchen, with breakfast and all.''

He shook his head. ''You won't be doing anything on this foot today, or for the week, probably. Maybe we should have Beau take an X ray. It could be fractured.''

''It isn't,'' she insisted. ''I can walk it off.''

She pushed him away before she did something really stupid, like drag him back onto the bed and... Well, beyond that, she couldn't think.

He glanced up at that instant. His hair was mussed, and one stubborn curl fell over his forehead. She swallowed hard as she recalled a time when she'd caught those shiny strands in her fists and pulled his lips to hers.

Her eyes locked with his. His bare chest moved against her knee as he inhaled sharply.

She realized he must have seen the blatant hunger that had swept through her at his touch, and she quickly looked away. She wasn't sure which pained her the most—the sprained ankle or the need that twisted her insides into knots.

A door slammed in another part of the house.

''Marta's here,'' Amelia said, relieved. ''I have to go.''

''Give me ten minutes,'' he requested.

When he grabbed his duffel and headed for the bathroom, she hobbled out of the suite and down the hall to the kitchen. Her ankle wasn't so bad, she decided. She could handle standing on it.

"What happened to you?" her helper asked, already mixing muffins to go in the oven.

"Tripped," Amelia reported wryly.

"Huh, maybe you'd better take it easy today," Marta suggested. "I can get the stuff on the buffet."

Amelia shook her head. Wonderful smells were coming from the oven, where cinnamon apples had baked to perfection. She'd put them in the night before and set the timer so they'd be ready that morning. She loved the way they scented the whole house and brought her guests hurrying to the great room to sample the simple but delicious fare.

After making a cup of tea, she slipped on mitts and did fine getting the baking dish out of the oven. But when she turned and stepped forward, pain shot up her leg, so harsh she gasped aloud. Her ankle gave way.

Hands closed over the mitts and steadied her until she could set the dish on the counter. "I told you to stay put," Seth snapped, his dark eyes shooting sparks at her.

"Seth Dalton?" Marta said, looking from him to the hallway behind him. There was only one bedroom in that wing of the house.

"In the flesh," he said in that same snarly tone. "Sit here," he told Amelia, practically tossing her onto a stool and yanking off her shoe, only to throw it aside in one fluid motion. "Where's some ice?"

Marta pointed wordlessly.

Grabbing a dish towel, he filled it with ice chips, then wrapped it around Amelia's ankle, ending by tying another around the whole. "There," he said.

Amelia stared at her foot in consternation. "I can't work with this on."

"Good. Because you're not going to."

With that, he lifted her from the stool, carried her to the sofa in the great room, placed her on it, removed her other shoe and carefully propped both feet on a velvet pillow. He grabbed a chenille throw from the shorter divan, gave it a shake and settled it over her legs.

After giving her a threatening scowl that told her she'd better stay put, he turned on the gas to start the logs in the large fireplace burning.

"Anything else you need?" he demanded.

She shook her head.

"Breakfast," Marta called out, observing all this from the kitchen doorway.

He nodded. "I'll take care of it."

Feeling utterly stupid, Amelia stayed where she'd been plunked and wondered what she'd done to deserve this. Her ankle throbbed fiercely, the icy coldness added its own ache, and she felt really, really wretched.

"Marta says you drink tea."

A cup was thrust under her nose. She took it, but not before giving the overbearing Samaritan a glare.

He grinned and disappeared into the kitchen. For the next half hour, Amelia watched as he brought out trays filled with muffins and loaves of Marta's special breads, as well as bowls of fruit and yogurt, jars of homemade jams and jellies and the baking dish filled with apples. Soon the sideboard, which she used to let her guests help themselves buffet-style, was filled. Coffee, tea and juice were placed on a granite-topped table close by.

Right on time at six-thirty, breakfast was ready. Seth went into the kitchen and returned with a tray, which he placed across Amelia's lap. The cook followed at his heels and gave Amelia a significant glance before handing him a second tray. Marta headed back to the kitchen while Seth hooked the rung of a chair with his foot and pulled it close to the sofa.

"Ahh, delicious," he said, using his fork to cut off a bite of baked apple, and eating it with relish. "Aren't you going to eat?" he asked, seeing her watching him.

Amelia picked up her fork. "I usually just have fruit in the morning."

"You could stand to gain a pound or two," he advised.

Huh, that was easy for him to say. If he only knew how hard she worked to keep the weight off!

But the scrambled eggs looked perfect, as did the sourdough English muffin, which Marta knew she loved. Not to mention the apple oozing with butter and sugar and cinnamon and sitting on a square of flaky crust. After the first bite, Amelia was lost. She cleaned up everything on the plate.

Seth removed the tray and refilled the teacup

without a word, although one black eyebrow did arch upward a bit in a superior male manner. He checked the amount of melting in the ice pack on her ankle, gave a grunt that she assumed meant it was okay, and left to assist Marta.

For the next three hours, he kept the buffet supplied, her ankle iced and her cup full. Amelia hardly noticed the ache as guests came and went, all of them sympathetic over her fall, their curious glances going often to Seth as he returned to her side between every chore.

When the meal was over and the nature lovers were out hiking in the blustery wind, since, fortunately, the rain had stopped, she dropped off to sleep, content for the moment.

Shortly after noon, Beau Dalton entered the B and B, black doctor's bag in hand. It didn't take a lot of smarts for Amelia to know why he was there.

"Ah, the patient," he said, smiling as he spotted her lying on the sofa like the heroine of a novel.

"Hi. I didn't know doctors made house calls anymore. Or still had black bags, for that matter."

He waved the bag at her. "Sure, that's what makes us official." He glanced hopefully toward the empty buffet table. "I was promised lunch if I stopped by. Got any of those baked apples left?"

Seth came out of the kitchen. "I saved you one, but it was a struggle. I had to arm wrestle two paying guests for it."

"I'll remember you in my will," Beau promised.

He came to Amelia and lifted the chenille throw. ''Let's see what the problem is with this ankle.'' He whistled appreciatively when he saw the bruising.

''Bad, huh?'' Seth asked, squatting beside his cousin.

Amelia waited anxiously for Beau's diagnosis. He probed gently, moved her toes, tickled her instep by running his nails lightly across it, then studied the bruising again. Opening the bag, he removed a stretchy bandage and proceeded to wrap her ankle securely, making her whole foot nearly immobile. And impossible to fit into a shoe.

''Not bad at all, considering,'' the doctor announced when he finished. ''Keep the ice on it today and tomorrow. That's held the swelling down nicely and will speed the recovery better than anything. As a nurse, I'll give you a recommendation anytime, bro,'' he told Seth. ''In fact, I could use someone in the office.''

''Huh.'' Seth only grunted in response to this amused suggestion.

''As for you,'' Beau said, turning back to Amelia. ''Stay off the ankle for at least a week, then take it easy about getting back to work. If it isn't better by Monday, stop by for an X ray. Listen to your body,'' he advised. ''In a few days, we'll start you on some physical therapy exercises so the joint doesn't permanently tighten up on you. Six months and you'll be as good as new.''

''Six months!'' She was aghast. ''I can't lie around for six months. I have a ton of work to do.

Honey and I are going to remodel the carriage house this winter.''

Honey was married to another Dalton cousin and rented the carriage house for a dance and exercise studio.

''No way,'' Beau said quite cheerfully. ''You can't lift drywall or anything heavier than a mop bucket for the next several weeks. You've pulled some ligaments and it'll take time for them to heal. If you're careful and do the exercises, you'll be fine. If not...''

Amelia felt her spirits sink as Beau shrugged, indicating it was up to her. Money was an issue. She'd managed to break even after three years and had made a profit during the four years since then, but it wasn't a big profit. Other than part-time help, she did everything herself, which was how she'd been able to survive.

''She'll do exactly as you tell her,'' Seth said in his no-nonsense manner. ''It was my fault she fell. I left my shoes beside the bed, and she tripped on them.''

A beat of silence followed this statement. It wasn't until Beau glanced from his cousin to her, humor and speculation rife in his gorgeous blue eyes, that Seth's words—and their implication—dawned on her.

''No,'' she quickly corrected, ''he didn't mean... It wasn't like that.''

''Right,'' Seth chimed in. ''I meant the sofa, not

Amelia's bed. I left my shoes by the sofa in her sitting room, not her bedroom."

"I understand." Beau bent forward and closed the black bag, but Amelia knew he was hiding a smile.

"All the rooms were full, so Seth slept on the sofa bed in my sitting room," she explained.

"It was late when I arrived," Seth added, "so I thought I would stay here rather than go out to the ranch in the storm."

"I tried to sneak out without disturbing him this morning," Amelia continued, "but without a light on, I didn't notice his shoes. I tripped and fell right on top of him."

"Scared me out of a sound sleep. I thought I was being attacked and grabbed her, pinning her to the mattress. I didn't realize she was hurt."

Beau grinned openly. "Not a bad way to wake up—having a beautiful woman fall into your bed and your arms. I'll mention it to Shelby."

The doctor had recently gotten engaged to his nurse. With two Daltons married and a third engaged, Amelia knew their uncle Nick was pleased. He planned on getting them all settled before he kicked the bucket, as he so delicately put it. At the thought, her eyes went to Seth.

He was looking at her, too. As clearly as if she could read his mind, she knew he was recalling those moments when, surprised out of sleep, he'd rolled her under him, his strong masculine body covering hers like a living shield, holding her there while his consciousness caught up with his instinctive self-protective reaction.

A tremor assailed her as she also relived those breath-stealing moments. The intimacy of the early morning hour. The mussed bed. The sleepy warmth of his body. The hardness that pressed into her abdomen. The excitement that had drummed through her. And through him.

"Where's that lunch?" Beau demanded.

"I'll get it." Seth went into the kitchen and returned with a loaded tray. He served soup, made by Marta before she left, and tuna salad sandwiches. He gave Amelia a big glass of milk and told her to "drink up" when she asked for tea, as if she were a child who needed the extra nourishment.

"You're in for it now," Beau warned her. "When Seth takes you under his wing, there's no escape. He'll boss you around and drive you nuts until you realize he's relentless. It's best to just give in from the first."

"Yeah?" Seth challenged. "The way you guys do when I suggest ways to maximize your savings and minimize your taxes?"

Beau rolled his eyes heavenward. "A dollar a week isn't a reasonable amount for spending money."

Amelia listened to the affectionate give and take between the men while they finished the meal. She'd once wished desperately for a family like that. She'd been twelve before she'd accepted that it was never going to happen. She was always going to be the only child of parents who argued over every decision, every turn in their marriage.

"Enough of this frivolity," Beau declared shortly, glancing at his watch. "Time for me to be back at work."

After he left, Seth cleaned up their dishes, then disappeared for a few minutes. When he came back, he hoisted Amelia into his arms. She instinctively flung her own arms around his neck and held on.

"Where are you taking me?" she demanded. Her voice came out husky instead of stern.

"To bed." He grinned and raised one thick black eyebrow in challenge. His eyes, so close now, met hers briefly, then returned to the hallway. "Time for your nap."

She found that the sitting room had been put to rights and the gas logs blazed merrily. He placed her on the restored sofa with a pillow under her head, then fluffed the blanket he'd used during the night over her supine form.

"Sleep," he suggested, his voice also husky.

She hesitated, then said, "Thanks for your help this morning. I never would have made it."

"No problem. Yell if you need me."

He left her alone in the sitting room, which had been her grandparents' bedroom during their fifty-six years of marriage.

The African violets on the windowsills were a personal legacy from her grandmother. Gran had loved the flowers, and Amelia did, too. They were the one thing she prized and took infinite care in growing. They rewarded her efforts with profuse blooms.

Like children, she thought, they thrived under loving care. That part of her life was empty, and she wondered if she missed it. She'd planned on having two or three or even four kids so they wouldn't be lonely.

As she'd been lonely?

The question pinged around inside her like a ball ricocheting off the walls of a handball court.

Yes, she admitted with a yawn. Vagabond children, sent hither and yon at what seemed like the whim of adults, were always lonely.

''No, I'll stay here until I can get things settled,'' Seth said into the telephone.

''The accident was your fault?'' Uncle Nick asked.

''Yeah. As you often told us—don't leave your things out so others will trip over them. I left my shoes in the way and Amelia stumbled over them. Beau says it's a bad sprain. Pulled ligaments can take up to a year to mend.''

''You're going to stay there and nurse her for a year?''

Seth frowned impatiently at the gleeful mischief in his favorite relative's voice. ''Of course not. However, it makes sense for me to stay in town while I'm establishing an office here. The B and B is perfect for that.''

There was a pause on the other end of the telephone line. "I'm glad you're coming home," Uncle Nick told him, "but is this a good time, what with the economy in a bad way and all? CNN reported the stock market was down again."

"Well, I'm starting slow," Seth reminded the older man. "I'll work Thursdays and Fridays in the office I'm setting up at Beau's place, and stay in the city Monday through Wednesday while I see how it goes."

Uncle Nick gave his approval. "Good thinking. Sharing expenses at the office should help a lot."

"It will." Seth checked the time. "I've got to call my law partner in Boise, see Beau about the office, then it'll be time for the social hour here. A man's work is never done," he quipped, then said goodbye and hung up.

He finished his business calls, then went quietly to Amelia's private quarters. Yep, she was sleeping like a cherub on the sofa, which was a lot more comfortable than the Victorian one in the great room.

He realized she would be in the house alone and asleep if he left. The doors of the B and B weren't locked during the day, so that guests could come and go freely. He tried to decide what to do.

After a moment, he smiled in exasperation. It wasn't like him to hesitate. He settled upon the best course and got on with it. However, he had to admit this woman had given him pause last night and this morning.

When she'd let him in, wearing a soft pink velvet

robe and fuzzy house slippers, he'd been rather taken aback by her appearance. This morning she'd fallen into his arms like a dream come true. His body had responded with rampant hunger. He hadn't been able to disguise that fact while he'd had her pinned beneath him, her gaze startled, then wary.

Now, lying on the sofa, her hair like banked embers spread over the pillow, she looked like Sleeping Beauty awaiting her prince.

And that wasn't him.

If ever there was a mongrel of dubious breed, he was it. Had Uncle Nick not vouched for him as a boy, today, as a man, Seth would probably be rotting in prison somewhere, resentful of life and what it had done to him. Nicholas Dalton had been his salvation.

Seth knew what a break he'd gotten. He'd been a stray mutt, taken in and fed and treated kindly. Never in a million years would he betray the trust Uncle Nick had shown in him.

He shook his head slightly, not sure what had brought on these deep, morbid musings. He had things to do. Going out the back door, he followed the sounds of music to the carriage house. There he found Honey, dressed in a black, full-body leotard, leading an exercise class.

When the music ended, she came over to him, wiping her damp face with a towel. ''Whew, it's getting hot today.''

''Depends on what you're doing,'' he said, taking

in the mix of overweight men and women. "Interesting class."

She glanced at the people preparing to leave. "It's something Beau thought of for his patients. For weight control and also flexibility."

"I see. Are you going to be around for a couple of hours?" he asked.

"Yes. Why?"

He explained about Amelia and her ankle, including the full details about why it was his fault, so that there would be no speculation about the situation. "So I need someone to keep an eye on her and the house while I'm out," he concluded. "She's asleep now."

Honey's eyes sparkled when she heard the story. "I don't have classes again until school is out at three. I'll be glad to stay with her."

"I'll be back in plenty of time to take care of the evening snacks." He frowned. "I'll have to order something for her dinner."

"Why not serve pizza? It's great for snacks or a meal," Honey suggested. "Don't tell Beau I said that, though. He's on a campaign to make people eat healthier foods."

"Good idea. I'll order several kinds from the Crow's Nest. And we can have fruit and veggies with it. You and Zack want to join us?"

"That would be lovely. I'll call and leave word at the office. He's off hunting down some poachers."

Zack was a deputy sheriff with the county, heading an investigative unit charged with solving mysterious crimes, such as who occasionally slaughtered a cow on the range. That had happened pretty steadily all summer. The local ranchers were furious.

Seth left Honey in charge of Amelia and the B and B while he drove to the equally large Victorian that housed Beau's medical practice and his own soon-to-be law office. Carpenters were working in the former dining room and parlor there.

Seth checked their progress, okayed a couple of minor changes in the plans, spoke briefly to his cousin, inviting him and Shelby over for the pizza dinner, too, then headed back to the B and B shortly after three, when Honey had to go back to her dancing classes.

Amelia was awake and on her feet when he walked in on her, surprising her in the kitchen.

''What the heck are you doing?'' he demanded.

She eyed him coolly. ''I have to plan something for tonight.''

''Didn't Honey tell you it's all been taken care of?''

She shook her head. Her hair was pulled tightly back into a ponytail. It refused to be tamed, however, and bounced jauntily each time she moved. She hopped on one foot to the refrigerator and removed a large tray. He saw she'd already prepared vegetables for the evening. That made him see red.

''Dammit, I turn my back for a minute and you're

up, disobeying orders and probably ruining your ankle.''

She gave him a look that said she doubted it.

Really irritated now, he removed the tray from her hands and set it on the counter. Next he swept her into his arms, toted her into the living room and plunked her on the sofa.

''Stay put,'' he warned when she made a move to rise.

She settled down, but not before glaring at him. The telephone rang. ''Well, are you going to take care of my business or not?'' she asked sarcastically.

The office was built into an alcove that had once been a closet under the stairs. Like the kitchen, it had Dutch doors, the top part open and tucked out of the way. He leaned over the bottom section and picked up the portable phone.

''Uh, Lost Valley Bed and Breakfast,'' he said, remembering the name of the place.

A woman asked about rooms and rates.

''Just a moment and I'll transfer you to the reservation clerk.'' He carried the phone to Amelia, who was still glaring his way. He grinned and dropped it into her lap, then headed for the kitchen to add the broccoli she'd prepared to the veggie selections.

Munching on a baby carrot, he finished filling the sections of the tray, placed the top over it and returned it to the refrigerator. When Amelia finished her conversation, he called the restaurant and ordered the pizzas. He gave his name and told the girl he'd pick them up at six.

''Five-thirty,'' Amelia called from the living room.

''Five-thirty,'' he corrected. ''You got bionic ears?'' he asked after hanging up.

She surprised him with a grin.

He made each of them a cup of tea and settled in a chair after adding logs and rekindling the fire. Now that the sun was going down, the air was cooling rapidly. He realized he loved the warmth of Indian summer days and the coolness of the nights.

''Ah, the good life,'' he said. Surprised, he realized he meant it.

Glancing at Amelia, he regretted that he wasn't the prince of her dreams. He hadn't been all those years ago when passion had nearly overwhelmed them, and he wasn't now.

That was an absolute fact.

Chapter Three

The great room of the B and B rang with laughter that evening. Amelia sighed contentedly. This was the best part of the day for her—when everyone was safely inside after a fun day of hiking and enjoying nature.

Her gaze was constantly drawn to Seth, who was checking the buffet over with the care he'd take with a supreme court case. Apparently satisfied that everything was in order, he turned, caught her gaze and waggled his eyebrows playfully. His grin was sudden, brilliant and pleased.

Her heart leaped around like a hungry deer spying a new meadow to graze. She shifted as longing blazed through her, and accidentally put pressure on her ankle. The throb of pain brought her back to the real world with a thud.

Being with him most of the day was interfering with her thinking processes. Seth would probably stay with her tomorrow, but on Monday he was due back in his Boise office.

What would she do then?

Marta could probably handle the breakfast alone. She'd be rushed, but she was competent. Preparing the guest rooms was the problem. Amelia did those, a task she enjoyed, as odd as that sounded to most people.

Each room had a different theme based on the natural trees and vegetation in the area. She often cut branches from the pines, cedars, firs, yews and oaks to add a touch of the outdoors throughout the house. From the garden, there were abundant fall flowers in a rainbow of colors to be arranged in tall vases and displayed in the living room and hallways. Who would handle all that?

"Ready?" Seth asked.

"For what?"

He scooped her up as if she weighed next to nothing. "Dinner," he replied.

He carried her down the hall to her sitting room. Three different kinds of pizza were there, along with a smaller platter of fresh vegetables and fruits. Before she could question this bounty, the back door opened.

"Hi, did I see boxes of pizza arriving a few

minutes ago?'' Honey asked. ''Zack's on his way. He said to tell you he was starved.''

''We're having company,'' Seth explained when Amelia raised a questioning gaze to his.

He put her in the rocking chair and moved a stool close so she could prop her foot up. After checking his watch, he decided it was time for another ice pack and headed for the kitchen, leaving the two women alone.

''How's your ankle?'' Honey asked.

When Zack Dalton, on an official trip to Las Vegas as a deputy sheriff earlier that summer, had brought home this mysterious stranger, gossip had sizzled through the local grapevine. It was further fueled by a to-do involving Honey and the cops. Then there'd been a quick marriage—family only—in Los Angeles, where Honey's brother apparently worked in some unknown but hazardous occupation. Rumor had it he was with the FBI or CIA or something like that.

Since then, the busybodies had watched Honey's waistline to see if it was increasing. It wasn't. She now crossed the room and took a seat on the sofa near Amelia, her movements supple and smooth as befitted a trained professional dancer. Honey held classes in the carriage house behind the B and B, an arrangement that benefited both of them.

Amelia grimaced. ''Fine…as long as I don't forget and try to move it.''

From the hall came greetings from a variety of voices. She recognized Seth's deep baritone and

Zack's. They greeted Beau, the doctor, and Shelby, his nurse and fiancée.

The Dalton men seemed of a marrying mind of late, she mused. The group entered her sitting room, bringing the crispness of the autumn air with them.

"I can't believe how cold it's getting, and it was so warm today—sixty-five by the thermometer on the porch at the clinic," Shelby was saying. She gave Amelia a sympathetic smile and handed her a gift bag.

Amelia removed two novels from the colorful bag and thanked Shelby for her thoughtfulness.

"So how are you doing?" Shelby asked, gesturing toward the injured foot.

"It's fine, really. Seth hasn't let me lift a finger all day. I may get used to a life of leisure," she said, tossing a warning glance his way.

"Beau said you tripped over Seth's shoes, which he'd left by the bed." Shelby raised her eyebrows, then grinned.

"What?" Zack interjected. He eyed Seth, Amelia, then Seth again. "Something going on that y'all want to tell us about, cuz?"

"No." Seth passed out paper plates, then started the pizza boxes moving. "Amelia doesn't approve of paper plates, but since I'm the one doing the dishes, I decided to use them, anyway."

"Good thinking," Beau murmured, struggling with laughter. He and Zack winked at each other while the other two women looked at Amelia with interest.

She could feel the heat rising to her face and hoped she didn't resemble a ripe cranberry.

"You guys knock it off," Seth ordered, but in amused tones. He placed a plastic bag filled with crushed ice on her ankle, then told Zack how he happened to be at the B and B and about the accident early that morning.

"I've spoken to Marta about help," he said to Amelia, taking the chair next to the rocker. "She says her cousin can come in next week and take care of the rooms. All you'll have to do is handle the phone. You can do that from the sofa, can't you?"

Five pairs of eyes turned to her.

Amelia could only nod. Decisions were being made, she was being consulted, but for some odd reason, she felt as if she were sinking in a quagmire. It scared her. Which was totally insane.

"Thank you," she said briskly. "That should take care of everything until I'm back on my feet."

Seth asked about her preferences, then placed slices of warm pizza on her plate. He and Zack went to the kitchen and returned with beer and sodas for everyone. She wondered how he knew she liked ginger ale rather than cola.

A chill ran over her, causing a slight shiver. Goose bumps sprang up on her arms.

"You're cold," Seth said. He covered her legs with the blanket and settled into the chair beside her again.

For the next two and a half hours, the three couples chatted about all the projects they were doing.

Zack assured Honey he would have time to help her with insulating the carriage house for winter. Seth and Beau agreed the new law office would be completed within six weeks. They would plan for a grand opening next month.

Work was continuing on a lodge the Daltons were building on the shore of the Lost Valley reservoir. Shelby and Beau had plans to remodel a cottage next door to the lodge, while Zack and Honey had bought a piece of property north of them, also on the lake, complete with an old farmhouse that needed restoration.

"You've done a wonderful job here," Honey complimented Amelia, indicating the B and B. "Perhaps you could help us with the plans for our house."

"If we ever get started," Zack added wryly. "With so many projects going on and the horse sale coming up, it'll be next year before we can even think about it."

Honey agreed. "I love staying at the ranch," she told Amelia. "Zack lets me help exercise his precious cow ponies, so I've come a long way with my riding skills. I'll probably cry when they're sold next month."

The Dalton ranch was known for its cutting horses. The upcoming sale would draw ranchers from several states, all seeking a chance to bid on the well-trained ponies. Amelia knew Zack and his twin brothers, Trevor and Travis, were instrumental in that expert training and that sale attendance was by invitation only, a sort of black-tie affair among ranchers, only they wore boots and ten-gallon hats as their formal attire.

''You've never been to a sale, have you?'' Seth asked.

Amelia shook her head.

''You'll have to spend the weekend with us at the ranch. There'll be games like horseshoes, plus roping, a shooting competition and the cutting horse trials. I personally enjoy the spitting contest the most, although Trevor is the best and always wins.''

The three men laughed, while the women looked dubious.

''When is Trevor due back from the rodeo circuit?'' Seth continued. ''He's been gone longer than usual.''

''He called last night,'' Zack replied. ''He stove in a rib, so he's going to a stock sale in Texas, then will come on home after that.''

They discussed changes to the beef herd and the problems of ranching, then of business in general, given the economic difficulties of the times.

Later, after the two couples left, Amelia yawned and stared dreamily into the fire. It had been a wonderful evening. Once upon a time she'd imagined life could be like that—

''Here,'' Seth said.

She took two pills from him and a glass of water. ''What are they?''

''Painkillers. Beau left them for you.''

She took them gratefully. ''Was I groaning or

something, so that everyone knew my ankle was hurting?''

''No, but you became more and more silent. I figured that was a good indication. Not that you tend to chatter at any time,'' he added.

She wasn't sure if that was a compliment or not, so she simply nodded, took another drink of water and carefully stood. Checking the clock, she was surprised to find it was well after ten.

''My, how time flies,'' she murmured.

''Where are you going?'' he demanded.

''To bed.''

He nodded and hoisted her off her feet.

''You can't carry me everywhere,'' she protested. ''I can manage. I need to go to the, uh—''

''The bathroom?'' he finished for her.

She nodded.

He deposited her at the door and closed it. She brushed her teeth and washed her face, then rubbed lotion on. Her good leg was starting to ache from keeping all her weight on it each time she hopped to the phone or bathroom or whatever when Seth wasn't looking.

She sighed, thinking of the work ahead. Seth couldn't be there every minute until she healed. She would have to cope as best she could.

A knock at the door startled her. ''Yes?''

''Here's your gown and robe.''

The door was opened a crack and the items thrust inside. She took them and quickly changed, folding her clothing neatly, with her underwear inside. She opened the door and peered out as if afraid of being attacked by wolves. Before she could take a step, he lifted her off her feet and placed her on the bed, which had the covers turned back, all ready for occupancy. He laid her clothing on a chair and turned back to her.

She swallowed hard as an ache of a different kind started inside her. Keeping her eyes averted from his face, so close to hers as he tucked her legs under the covers, she wished they were lovers and that he would be getting into bed with her, that he'd hold her close all night and make the pain go away with his sweet, hot kisses…

Forget it, she ordered her wild imagination. Forget that he'd ever held her and kissed her as if the world might end before he ever saw her again.

For her, it had. She'd been called home the next day. Her parents had actually divorced that winter, and her mother had decided she needed her daughter around for support. For all her parents' quarrels, Amelia had never thought it would come to that.

Oddly, her mom and dad had then got back together that spring. Amelia had returned to her grandparents while they honeymooned. All had been sweetness and light during the summer. Then they'd had another quarrel. That fall, she'd again moved in with her grandparents while she finished her senior year at high school.

Seth hadn't contacted her when he was home from the university. Not that she'd expected him to.

A vagabond kid wasn't exactly a reliable companion.

''Good night,'' he told her now, interrupting the memories by helping her out of her robe and laying it aside. He glanced around to see that she had everything she needed, then nodded and left.

She lay there with the lamp on for a while and listened as the wind blew mournfully from He-Devil Mountain. For the first time in seven years, she felt adrift. Her foot throbbed like a toothache, and she was filled with restless needs she tried to ignore.

From the next room, she heard the soft noises as Seth prepared the sofa bed.

Where can we go? he'd asked on a magic night long ago.

The carriage house, she'd answered, ready to follow him anywhere.

She wished they could go back to that night, to the innocence and heart-tugging sweetness of it, when she'd first realized the power and joy of falling in love.... That first sweet, glorious love...

Ah, well, she thought, consoling her heart with the knowledge that what had to be, must be. She flicked off the light and determinedly closed her eyes.

Sunday was a repeat of Saturday. Seth took care of keeping the buffet supplied. By eleven, all the guests were gone. ''What now?'' he asked.

''That's it,'' Amelia told him, ready with a bright smile. ''I don't have anyone coming in until Thursday, so there's nothing that has to be done until then. Thanks so much for your help. I really appreciated it.''

One black, expressive eyebrow lifted in its usual sardonic manner. ''You trying to run me off?'' he demanded.

''Well, I'm sure you want to visit your uncle before you return to the city.''

''Yeah, I do need to see him. Uncle Nick fixes a great Sunday lunch. We'll go out there.''

''Uh, not me. I prefer to stay here.''

''Then I'll stay, too.''

This wasn't going as she'd planned. He was supposed to accept her thanks, then gratefully leave, knowing he'd done his best for her. ''When are you returning to Boise?''

He crossed his arms and studied her for a few seconds. ''I've arranged for my partner to handle those clients I couldn't reach yesterday. Otherwise, I've canceled my appointments and plan to spend the week here.''

She was appalled. ''Oh, no. You shouldn't have done that. You don't have to take care of me. Really.''

''Who else is going to?''

No answer came to mind. She hadn't prepared for a grilling or his determination to stay. Neither did she want to face another night with him in her sitting room. It was just...just too much.

''I'll be okay,'' she insisted.

''We'll see how you are tomorrow, then decide if you can be on your own.''

At his reasonable tone and resolute stance, she knew it was hopeless to argue—he'd made up his mind. But inside, she seethed with anger at his high-handed I-have-everything-under-control manner. It was so like a Dalton!

He lifted her from the Victorian sofa, his smile taunting. ''Go ahead before you explode, Red.''

Only her grandfather had ever teased her and her grandmother about their hair, which was really an auburn-brown rather than flaming red. Tears stung Amelia's eyes as she realized how much she missed them.

''What?'' Seth asked quietly, as if seeing her distress.

She managed a smile. ''It's been a long time since I've been called that.''

''I think I'm jealous of the man who brought that look to your eyes.''

''It—it was my grandfather,'' she stammered, startled by his statement and the darkening of his eyes.

''Ah,'' he said enigmatically. ''Where's your purse?''

''In my sitting room.''

Ignoring her protests, he retrieved her purse and a jacket, then took her outside to his vehicle, a silver pickup with four-wheel drive and a camper unit.

''Do you camp?'' she asked, buckling the seat belt once they were inside.

''Not since my teenage days.''

She eyed the well-worn truck. He'd had it since he got out of college, she knew. ''I thought lawyers drove BMWs and traded them in every other year.''

''You've been watching too many movies,'' he said wryly.

Propping her sore right foot on her left knee, she shut up and enjoyed the ride. The fall colors were splendid, especially the buttery-gold of the aspens, which lined the creeks and gorges in the mountains. In town, maples had been planted in nearly every yard, adding brilliant red and russet to the mix.

Amelia relaxed with an exhaled breath. Her granddad had told her to learn to enjoy or endure that which couldn't be changed. Glancing at her companion, she couldn't help but smile.

''What?'' he demanded, taking her by surprise.

''I decided to enjoy the ride, since there apparently isn't anything I can do to change it.''

''A wise philosophy.''

He flicked her a glance that caused her heart to speed up, and heat to gather deep inside her. The ache of desire was almost as painful as the ache of a sprained ankle, she found. And it wasn't one-sided.

He'd never in any way referred to that interlude of passion they'd shared so long ago, but the knowledge of it was in his eyes and in the unspoken awareness between them.

She stared out the window until they arrived at the Dalton homestead. As they drove through the entrance—a huge log mounted on two others over the gravel driveway—she saw his uncle Nick, his cousin Travis and Travis's new wife alight from a station wagon.

"I thought that must be some of the family in front of us," Seth said. "I saw their dust when they turned onto the ranch road."

He parked beside the car and came around to help Amelia out of the pickup. He shook his head when she declared she could walk, and lifted her.

"Amelia, glad to see you," his uncle said, coming over to them. "Seth called yesterday and told me about the accident." He clapped his nephew on the shoulder. "Glad to see you taking care of things. How's your foot?" he asked Amelia, spearing her with his intensely blue gaze, which contrasted so effectively with his silver hair and tanned skin.

"Fine, thank you," she said, shaking his hand.

He was a handsome man. Lean and erect, he had to be seventy or better. The lines on his face showed both the worries and the laughter he'd experienced. His wife had died in a car wreck years ago, shortly after the orphans had come to live with them, and his daughter had been kidnapped at the same time. Or so everyone thought. No trace had been found of the three-year-old since the accident.

Amelia identified with his grief. Losing her grandparents had been like having a large part of her own heart torn out by the roots.

Travis and Alison greeted her warmly, then went to their house by a short trail through the woods.

"Let's go in," Seth suggested. "She's not getting any lighter."

Uncle Nick, as everyone called him, laughed at this and led the way inside. Amelia was placed on a leather sofa and the TV turned on to entertain her while the two men went in different directions.

Seth reappeared in fresh clothing—jeans and a V-neck sweater in royal-blue. Other than the sweat-suit, he'd had to wear the same clothing he'd arrived in on Friday. He went into the kitchen.

She'd often wondered how they did things in this mostly bachelor household. There'd been only one girl among the six orphans, Seth's half sister, Roni. Soon it was obvious, as the two males finished preparations for lunch, that they were well used to working together, and that neither was a stranger to the ranch kitchen.

Fifteen minutes later, Travis and Alison arrived, each carrying an item. "Dessert," Alison said. "Pumpkin pie."

"And real whipped cream," Travis added.

Amelia said it sounded delicious. The couple had changed from their Sunday clothes to jeans and long-sleeved chambray shirts. Tall and fit, they were a charming pair, him with the nearly black hair and blue eyes of the Dalton gang, her with blond hair and smoky-green eyes.

As it had the previous day, time passed swiftly. During a meal of baked chicken and mushroom dressing—Uncle Nick promised Amelia the recipe—they spoke of politics and happenings in the state. Alison's father was running for governor and she reported all was going well there.

"Are you still helping with his campaign?" Amelia asked.

Alison had stayed at the B and B during the summer and the two had become friends. The younger woman now taught business classes at the county high school.

"I mostly write press releases. However, I've made two speeches, one before three hundred wives of retired state employees and another to a teachers' group," she said.

"But no more," Travis said firmly. "We're expecting an addition to the family in late spring."

There was a moment's silence, then Seth broke it with his hearty congratulations. "Hear that?" he demanded of his uncle. "You've finally gotten your wish. The future generation is now assured."

"Young smart mouth," his uncle grumbled.

The old man smiled and offered his congratulations, but Amelia noticed the tears he kept blinking away, and was touched by his emotion. When she and Alison looked at each other, they both had misty eyes, too.

They all lingered at the table, speaking of old times and the children who had been born on the family homestead. Oddly, Amelia didn't feel left out.

"I knew your grandfather well," Uncle Nick told her. "He was a good man and a good friend to all who knew him."

This accolade for her beloved relative pleased her.

When Seth declared it was time for her nap, she was both sorry and relieved to go. Her foot throbbed and her head ached, but there was a glow in her heart.

"I'm glad for Travis and Alison," she said on the return trip to town. "After losing his first wife, Julie, and their child, I was afraid he'd never recover."

"So were we," Seth admitted. "Fortunately, the work on a ranch doesn't stop for tragedies or anything else. That was his salvation, I think. He had to go on."

"Being here helped me," she said without thinking as they parked on the gravel apron in front of the B and B.

"You stayed with your grandparents a lot, didn't you?" he inquired as he carried her up the steps and into the house.

"I wanted to live here all the time, but my parents..." She stopped, unwilling to share the difficulties of her past.

"They split up off and on over the years, didn't they," he said in a tone that held no censure or contempt, only a statement of fact.

"Yes."

He took her to the sitting room and put her on the sofa, then lit the gas logs to drive out the slight chill. He sat in the easy chair, kicked off his shoes and stretched his feet toward the fire.

"That must have been hard on you, having to change schools so often." He paused to cover a yawn. "But then, you graduated as valedictorian of your class. Smart kid." He smiled.

Though half-closed, his eyes were on her, sexy and compelling and something more. Warm and admiring...

She gestured self-consciously. "I didn't have anything to do but study."

"I remember that," he said softly.

"What?"

"Your way of being candid when others would have lied rather than admit the truth. Like that night when you told me no one had asked you to dance."

She was catapulted back into the past and the Harvest Moon ball and the misery of knowing it was her last night in Lost Valley. Her mother had sent for her and Amelia had had to leave the next morning.

"Did you ever wonder," he murmured, "how our lives might have changed had we made love that night?"

Chapter Four

Amelia slept late Monday morning. She woke with a sense of urgency gnawing at her. No wonder. It was after seven, she saw when she peeped at the clock.

Flinging back the covers, she leaped out of bed…and immediately fell back on the mattress, her ankle sending shafts of pain up her leg. Tears sprang to her eyes and she had to grit her teeth until the ache subsided.

Finally she was able to rise at a more gingerly rate, hop to the shower and prepare for the day. There was no rush this morning, since she didn't have any guests scheduled in.

But there was a mountain of linens to wash and rooms to clean and dust.

Using the elastic bandage, she again wrapped her foot, after frowning at the bruising that had made its way all around her ankle. After some thought, she dressed in a knit outfit of blue slacks and top, applied sunblock and a light dusting of makeup, then added her grandmother's diamond stud earrings for no reason except she felt like wearing them today. For shoes, she had to settle on an old pair of soft moccasins, the only thing that would go over the thick bandage on her right foot.

When she emerged from her quarters, she heard Seth on the phone in the office. She limped down the corridor, hugging the wall for support, and ducked into the kitchen without being seen. There, she made a cup of tea.

Sitting on a stool, she ate a slice of pumpkin-nut bread with nonfat cream cheese and a banana, and made out a list of tasks that needed to be done.

Food was the first item. She could order in most things from the grocery. Not that the store had a take-out service, but one of the advantages of living in a small town was that people helped each other in a pinch. The manager would have someone collect and deliver the items to the B and B when Amelia explained the problem.

She wondered where Marta's cousin was. The woman was supposed to come in—

"Well, good morning," a masculine voice said, breaking into her planning.

She forced herself to look at Seth. He was dressed in khaki slacks and a sage-green T-shirt with a tan-black-and-green-plaid long-sleeved shirt over it, clothing that he'd brought back with him from the ranch yesterday.

He was handsome, assured and totally relaxed. She, on the other hand, was a bundle of nerves. His idle question about their brief but torrid episode all those years ago had kept her awake for hours.

"Like you said," she'd replied to his query, "we had other plans." Then she'd made as dignified an exit as she could while hopping on one foot.

He'd let her go, but she'd been aware of his eyes on her, their dark depths filled with an unusual moodiness, a sort of…unhappiness, until she'd closed the door between the two rooms. Later, she'd decided she'd imagined the emotions in him. After all, what did a Dalton have to be unhappy about?

"How are you this morning?" he asked as he filled his cup with fresh coffee.

"Fine."

"Good. Eat up. We're going to get that X ray."

"I don't need one. My ankle is much better."

"Liar," he said softly. "Beau's waiting." He looked over her shoulder. "We can stop at the grocery, too."

It did no good to argue with him. By the time they reached the medical clinic, Amelia was thoroughly put out with Seth Dalton and his high-handed ways.

"Be careful," he warned his cousin when he carried her inside against her express wishes. "She's ornery as a cornered buffalo this morning."

''I'll keep my distance,'' Beau said. ''Bring her in here.'' He led the way to the equipment room.

After examining the X ray, the doctor decided she had a possible hairline fracture along one bone. He put her in a ''soft'' cast that strapped on, and covered her right leg from her toes to just below her knee. Then he outfitted her with a pair of crutches. ''As ordered,'' he added upon finishing.

''Ordered?'' she questioned.

''Seth said you needed crutches, since you weren't going to stay off your foot.''

She realized this would free her personal Samaritan to go about his business. ''Good idea,'' she murmured.

However, she found that by the time they returned from the clinic and the grocery she was exhausted. Walking with the aid of crutches wasn't all that easy.

''You need to rest now,'' Seth told her. ''What's next on the agenda? I'll take care of it.''

''Where's Marta's cousin?'' Amelia asked fretfully, keeping the list to herself.

''Her kid woke up sick this morning. She won't be in. Sorry, I forgot to mention it.''

''Damn,'' she said.

He took the list and looked it over. ''Tell me where things go, and I'll put the groceries away.''

She thumped her way into the kitchen and sat on the stool while he stored the food. When he finished, he insisted she go to her sitting room and rest. She did so gratefully, but with an odd resentment, too. She felt like crying. As if that would do any good.

"You can go now," she told him from the sofa, smiling brightly as he covered her with the blanket. "That's all that really needs to be done today."

He stood gazing down at her much the way he'd gazed absently at the porch Friday night, as if lost in secret thoughts. "You're angry about something," he finally said. "Because you feel I'm butting into your affairs?"

She gaped at his perception, then regained her poise. "Not at all. You've been wonderful this whole weekend, but you must have a thousand things to do. I'll be fine. Really. There's no need to waste more of your time."

"It was my fault you fell."

The resentment flared. She realized she didn't want him to stay because he felt guilty.

Like he was going to stay because he couldn't bear to leave her? Some cynical part of her mocked the forlorn yearning that filled her chest, making it difficult to breathe normally.

"It was an accident," she corrected.

He hesitated, then said, "Rest now." He left the room and closed the door silently behind him.

She let her breath out slowly. Funny little tremors ran through her, as if she had a fever. She wished he hadn't arrived on her doorstep, needing a room for the night. That the night of the Harvest Moon ball hadn't happened. That she hadn't married a man she'd known for two weeks because he was dark-haired and dark-eyed and had reminded her of the man she could never, ever have.

Instead of leaving, Seth stripped beds and washed towels and sheets until every room was ready once more for occupancy. He learned that the peach linens went with the peach room and the colorful green striped ones went with the matching curtains in the "cowboy room" with its rustic white cedar furniture.

When she awoke from her nap, Amelia went to the office, bringing the books up to date and answering the phone. To her relief, he moved his things into the single bedroom in the east wing on the lower floor so she had her quarters to herself once more.

On Tuesday and Wednesday, he made two quick trips into the city, for court appearances in a divorce case and the settling of a will.

When she asked, he told her about the cases and what he'd learned of human nature during his ten years of law practice.

"Money," he said, "brings out the true savagery of the human animal. It's amazing what members of a family will say and do to each other over the stuff. That's why Uncle Nick has an estate plan and the rest of us have our wills in order. I made sure of that after the first estate battle I witnessed."

When Seth learned Amelia didn't have a will, he offered her the use of his software to write one up for herself on his laptop computer, which he'd brought back from his office in Boise.

"I don't have anyone to leave the B and B to." She shrugged at his keen glance. "My parents aren't interested in it. My dad will retire in two years and they plan to move to New Mexico."

"Someone will inherit your estate," Seth reminded her. "Your husband and children someday, but you need an interim arrangement in case you're in an accident."

"I'll think about it," she promised, knowing a will would be the last thing on her to-do list.

"Ha," he retorted skeptically.

She couldn't help but grin. He did, too.

On Thursday afternoon, Amelia went into the garden with the snipping shears. She left one crutch inside, since she couldn't handle both of them along with the flowers she planned to cut. However, bending over proved more of a task than she'd realized. She grew dizzy and had to stand upright so that she didn't fall on her head.

"Here, let me," Seth said, arriving at the house and finding her in the yard.

He had removed his suit jacket and tie and rolled his white shirtsleeves up his forearms. His hair gleamed like ebony silk. And his smile...oh, his smile!

The air was cool, but the sun was warm. The rugged peaks of the Seven Devils Mountains seemed only an arm's length away in the pure clarity of the sky.

A perfect day, she reflected, with an ache in her heart because perfection never lasted.

He took the snips from her. Under her direction, he cut mums of various colors until she had an armload.

"Enough," she said, laughing, barely able to see above the colorful blossoms.

The wind blew his hair into disarray as he knelt beside the flower bed. He snipped one more blossom, a vibrant golden mum, and stood.

"I've heard if a yellow flower is reflected when held under the chin of a female, it means she's a passionate woman," he said in a low, husky tone.

He held the flower close to Amelia's neck, then stooped a little to peer under her chin.

"Does it—" She stopped abruptly, realizing the question was a giveaway of the curiosity burning inside her.

"Yes, it reflects," he said softly. He brushed the petals against her skin. "But then, I knew that."

The rush of hunger was so strong, so sudden, it left her light-headed. Clutching the bouquet of blossoms, she managed to turn and take two steps before losing her balance and pitching to the side.

Strong hands were there to catch her.

"Steady," he said, holding her lightly, his body warm and solid against her back.

He removed the crutch from her right hand and encircled her waist, supporting her and the bunch of flowers as they made their way into the kitchen. She let herself lean into him, just a little.

Under her direction, he helped arrange the mums in vases and baskets, and placed them in the great room as well as two of the guest rooms.

''Beautiful,'' he said at one point, looking at Amelia.

She swatted him with a broken bloom that was to be discarded. They laughed together.

At eight that evening, the two couples arrived, bringing the cold in with them as they hustled from their vehicle into the house. Seth checked them in and served hot cider in front of the fire.

Amelia marveled at how quickly he caught on to the system as he accepted a credit card and ran it through the machine, then updated the computer; how easily he chatted with the clients, who were from southern California and had planned a fishing weekend for the men and treasure-hunting for their wives. He gave the women maps of antique and junk stores along the highway, mentioned a yard sale he'd noticed and the Native American store on the highway north of them.

''Your B and B is charming,'' one of the women said, glancing around the great room. ''I don't suppose any of the clocks in here are for sale?''

''No, sorry,'' Amelia said. ''My grandfather collected and repaired them. They aren't all that valuable, except to me.''

''I see.'' The guest glanced at Seth, then back to Amelia, envy in her eyes. ''Did you and your husband grow all these splendid flowers?''

''Yes,'' said Seth.

"No," said Amelia.

There was laughter from the couples. "Well, which is it?" one of the men asked.

"I have a gardener. He isn't my husband."

That brought more laughter and more confusion.

"Amelia owns this place and has a gardener who takes care of the grounds," Seth explained. "I'm helping out this week because of her sprained ankle."

"And what do you do normally?" the woman asked.

"A little of everything," he said with a wry smile.

"Seth is an attorney in Boise. His family has a ranch near here. He often comes up for the weekend," Amelia said.

He looked pensive. "I'm in the process of moving my offices here, a sort of coming home, if you will."

"Back to your roots," one of the men said. "I'd like to do that, but I work in electronic equipment development."

Seth nodded. "Boise has a growing technology industry and is less expensive and crowded than the coast."

"Mm, that might be worth checking into." The man covered a yawn and stood. "It's been a long day for us. I think I'll head to the room. Thanks for the cider. It hit the spot."

After the couples disappeared upstairs, Seth lifted Amelia and carried her to her bedroom. "Sleep tight," he murmured, setting her down and putting her crutches close to the bed. "I'll lock up before I go to bed."

She heard him moving around the house, checking the doors before he went to the small room with the single bed that was rarely rented unless a lone hiker showed up, as had happened last weekend.

She wondered where Seth would live when he got his office up and running here in Lost Valley. For a second, her heart set up a clamor, then subsided. Wherever he lived, it was none of her business.

None.

None.

After helping Marta with breakfast the next morning, Seth left to speak at a Chamber of Commerce luncheon about the future of the town. As a member of the business group, Amelia went with him. His uncle was also there.

"Is Seth taking proper care of you?" Nicholas Dalton asked her with a twinkle.

"Very much so." She handed Seth the crutches after she was seated. Recalling that he'd hardly let her do a thing all week, she added, "Maybe more than is necessary."

Uncle Nick laughed, obviously delighted, and took the chair beside her. "He's a good man. Some smart woman ought to grab him up."

Amelia knew about the older man's matchmaking ways. "I'm sure one will."

"It had better be soon, else I might not be around for the wedding."

Alarmed, she surveyed his lean, fit-looking form. ''Are you feeling ill? Do you have chest pains or anything?''

He snorted. ''No, but I'm not getting any younger, and neither is Seth. He turned thirty-four two weeks ago.''

''Uh, yes, I recall that.''

Uncle Nick leaned close. ''You could seduce him—perfect chance, him staying at your house and you being hurt and it being his fault and all.''

The blood rushed to her head so fast, Amelia was afraid she might keel over on the spot. She grabbed the chair seat and held on until the wave of shock passed.

''What's happening?'' Seth asked, taking the seat on her left and peering at her closely. ''Oh. Uncle Nick must have told you to seduce me.''

She went dizzy again.

''See what you've done?'' Seth demanded of his relative. ''You've embarrassed Amelia.''

Uncle Nick wasn't daunted. ''You should grab her up. She's a good-looking woman.''

''I agree. But she can do a lot better than a lawyer trying to make a living in an area full of stubborn ranchers.''

Several other members of the business organization had arrived and were openly listening to the argument. Amelia began to feel like the proverbial bone of contention between two equally determined canines.

''Marriage is far from my mind. I have a business

to run,'' she reminded them, hoping to change the subject.

''She's smart as well as beautiful,'' Seth said in admiring tones.

''Right,'' his uncle agreed, as the president of the group called for order. Leaning close, the old man whispered loudly enough for six people around them to hear, ''You don't have to worry. Seth is an honorable man.''

She wished she hadn't come to this meeting.

However, when Seth was introduced and rose to speak, Amelia felt a surge of unwarranted pride. Following it came an undefined heaviness of spirit, haunting her with longings she didn't understand and didn't want. She had no right to pride or any other emotions regarding him.

On Sunday, after the couples left, Seth prepared the bedrooms for the next influx of visitors, due the following Friday. This time the guests would be Shelby's family, coming up for her wedding to Beau Dalton over the weekend.

The whole town was excited about the nuptials of the handsome young doctor and his nurse. No wonder. It was the third Dalton marriage in six months.

Must be a virus going around, Amelia decided grumpily, waking at first light on Monday morning.

Seth was in the great room, drinking coffee and reading the paper, when she limped in on the crutches. ''You're up. Good. I wanted to see you before I left.''

Her heart did a double hitch, then settled down. She headed for the kitchen.

"Sit," he ordered. "I have breakfast ready."

He brought out toast and eggs and homemade jam, plus a glass of milk and hot tea for her. Taking his seat at the table, he told her all was in order with the B and B, reminded her she should think seriously about a will, and explained he had to stay in the city for the week, but would return Friday morning to help her handle the wedding guests.

"That's okay. Marta will help, and I can get around fine now."

"Don't argue," he said softly. "I'll be here."

"You Daltons always expect to get your way." Amelia's tone was resentful, and she didn't care.

"Not always." He smiled sardonically. "But we usually do." He took both her hands in his. "I booked the single room for myself. Keep it for me, you hear?"

She nodded, aware of his hands on hers. His palms had the calluses of a working man. She knew he'd worked all summer building a lodge over at the lake, and he'd helped finish the house for Travis and Alison before their marriage in August.

He had also gotten through college in three years, then through law school in another three years, by working construction jobs that had kept him out of town most of the time.

Seth's hardworking as well as honorable, she mentally told his uncle. Other than a superficial physical one, any resemblance of her youthful husband to this man had been a delusion on her part.

A mistake of the heart, she mused. It had been Seth Dalton she'd wanted. At this bit of wisdom, she smiled with nostalgic sadness and forgave the girl she'd once been for wanting what was never meant to be.

"What are you thinking?" Seth asked quietly.

She focused on his dear face, this fascinating, many-faceted man she had loved with her whole sixteen-year-old heart. "Of what might have been."

To her surprise, he cupped her face and gazed into her eyes for a few seconds before leaning closer and touching her lips with his. When he closed his eyes, she did, too.

The kiss was the gentlest she'd ever known and caused a rain of tears inside her.

When he lifted his head, he said enigmatically, "I'm not the person you think I am."

With that, he was gone.

She touched her lips as if she could feel the imprint of his kiss there. "Then who are you?" she murmured as she gazed at the mountains, magical in their autumn colors.

By Friday, Amelia's foot was so much better she asked Marta to drop the borrowed crutches at Beau's office on her way back from the grocery. With the support of the cast, she could walk without pain and get her work done.

The B and B was ready for the wedding guests,

who would arrive shortly. Shelby had planned a reception for them and the Daltons in the great room that evening, a sort of welcome and bridal dinner all in one, buffet-style.

"The flowers are lovely," Shelby said, placing a vase of fresh white mums and blue asters on a corner of the sideboard where the meal would be served.

The nurse had bright red hair with golden tones. It flowed like a shimmering curtain of flames straight down her back without a ripple. Her eyes were deep blue. Amelia knew that Shelby had been adopted and had come to Lost Valley looking for her birth mother.

Like Amelia, Shelby had married and divorced at a young age. She'd had a child who'd died from a genetic disorder, and had needed to find out if the trait ran in her birth family. It hadn't. Now she was free to marry Beau and start a new life with him and his own son.

Amelia sighed, happy for the couple. "I told the gardener we had to have special flowers for the wedding. I think he gave each plant a pep talk about what was expected of them this month."

"We're lucky to have nice weather this long." Shelby went to one of the tall windows that lined the south side of the room. "No snow, except for a dusting on the high peaks, and here it is—the first day of November."

"I'm glad you didn't choose Halloween colors. Pumpkins are nice, but not exactly a wedding staple. Mmm, they could be a fertility symbol, though. The grapevine gossips are keeping a sharp eye on the waistlines of any women associated with the Daltons.''

Both of them laughed and continued the preparations for the feast. It occurred to Amelia that the local busybodies might be keeping an eye on *her* as a result of Seth's staying at her place all the prior week. She almost wished there was a reason for their spying.

No!

An affair between her and Seth was out of the question. There was an attraction, but that was as far as it went.

Because of his caution, some sly part of her suggested. If it had been up to her, they probably would have made love years ago. Or last week.

She had to stop thinking about the possibilities, but, she had to admit, it was much more difficult now.

''There, everything's ready,'' Shelby declared. She clutched her hands together. ''So why am I suddenly scared to death that something is going to go wrong?''

''Bridal jitters,'' Amelia assured her friend. ''Tomorrow will be here before you know it, the wedding will be perfect and you'll forget you ever had a qualm.''

''I think I wish it was already over,'' Shelby said in mournful tones.

Seth and Beau entered the great room. Seth raised one eyebrow. ''You'd better do something, Doctor.

Sounds as if the bride is getting a bad case of cold feet. Not that I blame her,'' he added. ''Have you heard him snore?''

His joking had them all chuckling, and soon the two Dalton men were relating incidents from their wild and misspent youths. Zack arrived and joined the fun.

''No wonder you're nervous,'' Amelia said to Shelby with great sympathy after a tale involving a mean rancher and a giant pumpkin that the Dalton gang had placed on a stump and stuck their uncle's old hat on.

Thinking he'd caught a rustler, the rancher had blasted the criminal with rock salt from his shotgun and called the sheriff's department to report a bunch of thieves. Zack, being a new deputy, got the call. He'd rushed to the rancher's rescue and found his first big case was a pumpkin shot to smithereens, the gang of thieves all in the man's imagination. The story did earn a front page write-up in the local paper, though.

When Shelby's parents, aunts, uncle and cousins, plus the rest of the Dalton clan, arrived, the story had to be recounted. Other tales followed and the evening didn't end until almost midnight.

Amelia, after seeing that everyone had eaten and that dessert and fresh wine, coffee and tea were available, went to her room at ten. A knock on the door startled her.

''Yes?''

Seth identified himself, and when she opened the

door, came in with a tray. ‘‘I didn’t see you eat anything.’’

‘‘I wasn’t very hungry.’’

‘‘You were too busy seeing to everyone else.’’ He pushed the door closed and set the tray on the coffee table, then looked her over. ‘‘Why don’t you change clothes?’’ he suggested. ‘‘Then I’ll put an ice pack on your ankle. It’s probably swollen from all the standing you’ve done today.’’

She didn’t want to tell him that she’d overdone it and that her foot was aching with fatigue.

‘‘It won’t do you any good to argue,’’ he added after a brief silence. He headed for the door.

When she returned to the sitting room, he had the fire going, a pot of steaming tea ready and a plastic bag of chipped ice in his hand. ‘‘Sit,’’ he said.

Lifting her pink robe and nightgown out of the way, he removed the cast and cursed softly when he saw her ankle. ‘‘Little fool,’’ he chided, ‘‘don’t you know how to take care of yourself?’’

It was a rhetorical question, so she didn’t bother to answer. Instead, her will as weak as water, she let him take over and do as he wished. It felt so good to simply relax and let him have his way.

Chapter Five

Seth woke abruptly when a blue jay shrilled an angry caw outside the bedroom window. He couldn't recall the dream he'd been having, but he had a vague notion of confusion, turbulence and, from the state of his body, erotic doings.

The golden rim of the sun was just visible from his window when he rose, pulled on sweatpants and headed down the short hallway to the bathroom.

There wasn't a sound in the house. He liked having the early morning hours to himself—

Whoa! What was that?

A furtive creak of a floorboard halted him in his tracks. Stepping carefully to make sure he didn't alert the intruder, he paused at the entrance to the great room.

No one was there.

He noticed the light gleaming around the kitchen door and relaxed...if trying to control a wave of righteous anger could be considered relaxing.

Opening the sectioned door, he stood on the threshold and observed Amelia as she put the finishing touches on a pan of apples, then turned to put them in the oven. She visibly jumped when she saw him standing there.

"You scared me," she accused, bending and sliding the baking dish into the bottom oven.

"You're lucky I haven't decided to beat you," he told her in a near snarl. "Are you trying to permanently injure yourself?"

After closing the oven door, she faced him, her expression as deadpan as a poker player's. "I forgot to put the apples in last night."

There was more than a hint of defiance in her stance. When her gaze dropped downward, then snapped back to his face, he realized he wore nothing but the sweatpants, and she was still in her gown and robe and the fuzzy pink slippers so at odds with his view of her as a no-nonsense person.

"Are you finished now?" he asked in a much huskier tone.

She nodded. "Sorry I woke you."

"You didn't." But a misty image from his dream told him that maybe she had.

She'd been part of the confused turbulence, he now recalled. His partner. Hand in hand, they'd run down endless canyons while the mountains soared around them, keeping them trapped. At last they'd found refuge in a secret cave.

Alone and safe, they'd turned to each other, their kisses hot and urgent and as necessary as air. Then the screech of the jay had awakened him...

"I'm going to shower and change now," she said, and hobbled past him and down the hall to her quarters.

He retreated to his wing of the house, showered and dressed in casual clothing. At three, he would change into a suit and go to the small church the Dalton family had attended for more than a hundred years. There, Beau would say his vows with the lovely Shelby.

Returning to the kitchen, Seth found coffee already prepared in the big silver urn Amelia used when the house was filled with guests. Filling a tall mug, he retrieved the morning paper.

After looking over the headlines, he sat there in the early morning quiet, listening to the occasional groan of the old house in the light breeze blowing down the valley and sipping his coffee.

The Victorian represented home and family to its owner. That's why she'd returned and started the B and B. Amelia's roots were here, growing deep in the rocky soil with those of her grandparents. Emigrants from Europe, they had bought the old house, repaired it, then started a truck garden, taking vegetables to Boise to market, plus doing any odd jobs that they could find.

He considered his own roots. Until he was twelve

and had come to live with Uncle Nick, he'd had none. Meeting the Dalton twins, Job and Jed, and Jed's wife, at a rodeo had been the luckiest thing that had ever happened to him and his mom. When Job had asked them to come with him to the family ranch, they'd thought heaven had opened its doors.

"Deep, dark thoughts?" A soft feminine voice broke into his musing.

He mentally slammed and locked the safe containing his memories. "Nothing important," he said.

Amelia, dressed in sage-green slacks and a beige top with green-and-brown leaves embroidered on it, entered the kitchen and prepared a cup of tea. She wore moccasin slippers. Those, along with the blue material of the support apparatus showing below the slacks, were incongruous with the outfit.

She smiled. "I know. It looks funny."

"I'm surprised you can get anything on over the cast."

"Frankly, I was, too." She put on mitts and removed the apples, then mixed batter for pancakes.

Seth watched while she moved with an efficient limp around the kitchen, the remnants of the strange dream nibbling at the edges of his consciousness. Then, as if he'd been transported through time into the future, he could see her doing the same thing, but with a husband and children surrounding her, a loving part of her busy, contented life here in this sturdy old house.

A bitterness he hadn't felt in a long time washed

over him, ambushing his thoughts and the idyllic vision.

He would never be that loving husband, the caring father, the helpmate that this woman deserved.

Uncle Nick thought Seth was honest, but he believed the best of everyone until proved different. The old man had even lied for the twelve-year-old left in his care when Seth's mother had been killed in the avalanche.

And Seth had let him. He'd kept silent as Nicholas Dalton swore the boy was his brother's son, and signed papers to that effect. The county judge had believed him. Everyone had, for the Daltons were an old and respected family.

And so, by a stroke of misfortune and the goodness of one man, Seth Rodrigues Maguire of nowhere, a mongrel mix of Sioux, Hispanic, Irish and English, became Seth Dalton of Seven Devils Ranch, Idaho.

But he had never forgotten where he came from. That's why he knew he wasn't the man of any woman's dreams. Within him lived the seeds of his father, a dangerous, alcoholic liar and thief who'd served time in prison for manslaughter resulting from a drunken brawl over a poker game; a man who would as soon backhand his wife and son as smile at them; a mean, unpredictable man that Seth wouldn't wish on his worst enemy. Those were *his* roots.

"Take these to the buffet?" Amelia asked.

Seth realized others were up and moving about

the house. He carried apples and hot loaves of nut breads to the sideboard. He put out coffee, milk and tea. When the pancakes, eggs and sausage were ready, he added those along with a crystal bowl of fruit.

"Pretty fancy," he told her, returning to the kitchen to make sure she sat down and ate, too.

"I was afraid no one would get a chance to have lunch today with so much going on." She pushed a curl off her face. It promptly fell over her forehead again.

He tucked it into place, then lingered as tenderness overcame the last tinge of bitterness. "You're a thoughtful person and a good friend."

Emotion swelled in his breast, and he wanted to grab her up and find that hidden cave and live with her there, just the two of them, safe in a world of their own.

He closed his eyes for a moment, seeking sanity in the hot swirl of longing that engulfed his soul. He suddenly wanted to tell her everything, to have her know and understand and perhaps forgive…

The vows of his youth came to him. He'd vowed never to hurt anyone the way his father had hurt him and his mother. He'd vowed never to tell anyone who he was and where he came from and, most of all, he'd vowed that no one would know that Uncle Nick had put his own honor on the line and lied for him. So far, Seth had kept his word.

Opening his eyes, he saw Amelia watching him,

with that curious blend of patience and desire in her eyes.

"Sorry," he murmured, and backed off. Heaving a shaky sigh, he left the kitchen and went to join the laughing crowd in the great room.

Amelia was aware of Seth with every step she took. Beau and Shelby came over for breakfast with her family. Seth asked his brother to check her ankle again. In the kitchen, the doctor made sure the strap-on cast held her ankle immobile, which it did, then agreed with Seth that she was doing too much and should rest more.

"Rest and keep your foot elevated as much as possible," he advised.

She promised she would.

"Ha," Seth muttered in response.

"As soon as the wedding is over," she added.

Beau released her foot and gazed at her with his gorgeous blue eyes. "Shelby's nervous. I really appreciate all you've done to make things easier for her."

"It's a pleasure," Amelia assured him. "We've had fun working on Lost Valley Historical Society stuff since she moved here."

"You're a good friend," he said.

After he left, the kitchen was quiet compared to the great room, where Shelby's relatives were gathered. Amelia idly rubbed her brow, feeling a slight headache, then yawned as she realized how tired she was.

"You need to rest," Seth scolded.

Looking into his dark eyes, she wondered about his life before his father and mother had gotten together again. Apparently they'd had an affair long ago, before his dad met and married Beau and Roni's mom. Seth was four years older than Beau and eight years older than Roni.

That meant he'd been around twelve when his parents had died in the avalanche. Just when they'd found each other a second time. How terribly sad for them. And for the boy who'd been orphaned so soon after finding his father.

"Is your foot hurting?" Seth asked.

She realized something of her emotions must have shown on her face, and forced a smile. "Not at all." She rose. "We had better check the food supplies."

He pushed her back on the stool. "I'll check. You stay put."

She remained where she was and watched him replenish the buffet. They had both been vagabond kids, she realized. He'd never spoken of his early life, but she somehow knew it had been difficult and lonely. The way hers had been.

Invisible ties looped around her, reaching out to include him. She felt the connection like a gentle flow of autumn rain in her heart—sad, but also comforting at the same time. It would be easy to imagine herself in love with him.

The front door opened, bringing the scent of wood smoke from the many fireplaces in town.

"Miss Pickford," she heard Shelby say.

Miss Pickford was president of the Lost Valley Historical Society, which met each month at the B and B. She was also Shelby's cousin from her birth mother.

"Please call me Peggy Sue," Miss Pickford requested. "I brought someone I think you should meet. My cousin...your grandmother. She's waiting outside."

Silence fell over the group.

Realizing that Shelby might need some privacy to deal with the situation—after all, it wasn't every day that an adopted person met the mother of her birth mother—Amelia quickly limped into the other room. "Why don't you use my sitting room?" she said to Shelby.

Beau came over and put an arm around his fiancée. "Come," he said gently. "You'd better come, too," he said to Shelby's parents. "Please bring her inside," he said to Miss Pickford. He led the way down the hall.

After they disappeared into the sitting room, a subdued murmur rose from the other guests. Seth offered everyone more coffee. Amelia helped him clear the buffet.

"Now," he said, lifting her into his arms.

She clutched him around the neck. "What are you doing?"

"They may be a while in your room. You grimace each time you take a step, so you're going to rest."

Without paying the slightest heed to her protests,

he took her to his room and placed her on the day bed, which, to her surprise, he'd straightened.

"I thought men didn't know how to make up beds," she murmured, aware of flutters along her nerves. "My grandfather never made a bed. My grandmother never put gas in a car. She said it was an unspoken deal between them."

Amelia realized she was chattering and shut up.

Seth removed her moccasins and spread an afghan, one that her grandmother had crocheted, over her. He pulled down the blinds so the light was muted. Seeing the clock, she realized it was almost noon.

"I wonder if Shelby's parents feel threatened by a relative from her birth family showing up."

He stuck his hands in his pockets and paced the small room like a trapped panther longing for freedom. "It can be pretty confusing for everyone."

"Was that the way it was for you when your father suddenly reappeared in your life?"

He pivoted and sat on the side of the bed so suddenly, she was startled.

"What do you know of my father?" he demanded in a voice so harsh she recoiled in alarm.

"Only what everyone said—that he and your mother had found each other again after a long time and that he hadn't known he had a son."

"You're talking about Job Dalton."

It wasn't a question, but she nodded, anyway.

He breathed deeply and let it out slowly. "No, I wasn't confused. I'd already found out that adults did things that were incomprehensible and unpredictable.''

His smile did things to her heart. It reminded her of children who'd seen too much, too soon, in their brief lives, their expressions weary and resigned, the knowledge that their world was never going to change stamped on their young faces.

Unable to stop herself, she reached out to caress his cheek. He caught her hand, brought it to his lips and pressed a burning kiss in the palm. His eyes went fathoms deep as he stared at her.

It was as if his body remained but his soul had gone someplace else, a place of pain and forbidding darkness.

''Seth,'' she whispered, her voice tremulous with grief for that boy.

''You don't have to feel sorry for me,'' he told her softly, mocking her pity. ''My life turned out great.''

The raw agony in his eyes belied the words. ''Yes, it did,'' she agreed. She drew him into her arms, insisting with her touch that he yield for once.

Hunger rose in her, urgent and undeniable. ''Stay,'' she murmured, and pressed her face against his throat, afraid that he would see how deeply she needed him.

''We shouldn't do this,'' he said. But he didn't move.

''I know.''

The world stopped for a second.

She heard the soft thuds of his shoes on the carpet, then the rustle of the bed as he stretched out beside her. She felt the warmth of his body, then his arms as he embraced her. It was like coming into a safe haven.

They lay there together in the soft quiet of the room. No voices, no sounds of the outside world impinged on them. His lips touched the side of her neck, then moved upward, inch by inch, until he found her mouth.

Her lips trembled when he touched them.

He lifted his head and gazed into her eyes. ''I'm not promising anything. No tomorrow. No future ties.''

She barely moved her head in acknowledgment.

''I'm not the man you want,'' he finished.

She set him straight on that. ''Oh, yes, I do want you.''

He closed his eyes as if in pain, but when he looked at her again, only the flames of passion blazed there.

''I want you, too. God help me, but I do.''

This last was said with a low groan, the words seemingly pulled from the depths of his soul. She didn't know how to comfort him. ''It's okay,'' she whispered, then turned her lips to his, inviting his kiss.

Seth couldn't resist the sweetness of her mouth, the heat that warmed him clear to the bone, all the way to the cold secret place inside him that nothing could penetrate.

When she moved against him, making it clear she

wanted his caresses, his thoughts dissolved and time—the past, the present and the future—went away.

With a tenderness that was new in its depth and care, he explored her lithe body, finding her feminine form both fragile and strong.

''Mmm.'' She gave a purr of pleasure when he stroked her back and sides, her hips and thighs.

When he cupped her breast, she pressed forward, a kitten wanting to be petted. Beneath her clothing, he felt the tight beading of her nipple, and experienced an explosion of need that urged him to hurry…hurry….

He held back, basking in the growing heat between them, as if they'd ignited tiny blazing stars that burned just for them. He suddenly understood Uncle Nick's advice.

''Sometimes there's one person, just one, and she'll make your heart sing,'' the older man had told him. ''Save your heart for her. Don't accept another, lesser love.''

Seth shook his head slightly, pushing the words away and taking the gift of Amelia's passion. Tomorrow he might suffer, but for now, there was only her and *this.*

Amelia pushed aside the cloth that kept her hands from his flesh. She wanted to see him, touch him, have complete contact.

''This isn't enough,'' she told him, and tugged at his dark gold polo shirt.

''Easy,'' he whispered, but he let her pull the soft

knit over his head and arms and toss it aside. ''Now you.''

With a few rushed movements, her new autumn top sailed to a chair and draped gracefully over the arm. Her dark beige bra with its satin embroidery work soon joined it.

''Pretty,'' he said, with a slight smile. ''Beautiful,'' he added then, gazing at her bare torso.

She leaned forward and kissed his chest, liking the tickle of the thick patch of wiry hair. Next to her paleness, he looked like a buccaneer who spent his days in the sun, tanned and fit and in the prime of manhood.

''I want to know you,'' she said as desperation washed over her. ''I need to feel you, your flesh on mine....''

He eased away from her embrace and stood. ''You make my knees weak...just by looking at me...the way you are now.'' He breathed in gasps, as if he had run a hundred miles; he felt he could run a hundred more. ''Just keep looking at me like that.''

''Hurry,'' she pleaded, feeling barren without him.

''Your turn,'' he coaxed, coming back to her. He sat on the side of the narrow bed. Her slacks had elastic in the waist, so he had no problems with buttons or other hindrances.

She lifted her hips when he told her to, then her legs as he slid the offending clothing from her body.

The cool air bathed her in chills. ''Hurry,'' she said again.

''One more thing.''

He went to the door and clicked the lock into place, then crossed to the luggage stand and removed a small box, aware of her eyes on him every second.

''I didn't plan anything,'' he said, turning so she could see the box, ''but on the way here from Boise, when I stopped for gas, I went into the market.''

She nodded, and he knew she understood. He hadn't planned a seduction, but things were volatile between them. It was a man's duty to take care of his partner and not leave her any unwanted surprises.

Her watchful gaze made him as clumsy as a boy as he secured the condom. Meeting her eyes, he smiled. ''You do things to me,'' he said.

''You do things to me,'' she echoed softly.

A knot formed in his chest as he returned to her. Her cheeks were rosy, her lips full and tantalizing.

Something rare and painful clamored deep inside him, demanding to be let out. He didn't know what it was, but he knew the feeling. He'd had it one cool October night years ago when he'd walked a girl home from a dance and, lost in their kiss, he'd felt the stars falling around them.

He gazed his fill of her slender body. Her nipples were beaded, the shape and color reminding him of the wild raspberries he'd eaten as a boy. Her hair lay in a sweep of dark fire over the pillow. The color was repeated at the juncture of her thighs. "A true redhead."

It surprised him when she blushed. He observed the pink rush up her throat and join the rosy glow of her cheeks, and was spellbound by her beauty.

His blood surged hotly throughout his body. When she lightly stroked one hand down his thigh, he thought he was going to burst.

"Easy," he told her, lying next to her once more. "My fuse feels as if it's lit at both ends."

"I'm already down to cinders," she said, with a little laugh that delighted him.

She rose on one arm and lightly brushed the tips of her breasts back and forth across his chest.

"I have to have a taste," he said apologetically, and slid down until he could take her into his mouth.

Amelia gasped at the spirals of electricity racing through her as he nuzzled and teased her nipples until she trembled with need. "I want you," she gasped. "Now!"

"Not yet. I haven't had near enough of you."

He pressed her onto her back and proceeded to kiss her all over, circling her navel with his tongue, then making her laugh as he delved inside the shallow depression. The laughter died as his kisses became more intimate.

When he slipped between her thighs and strewed wanton kisses down to her knees and back up, going slower and slower, driving her insane, she stopped breathing and hung suspended between one moment and the next, completely in his grasp and loving it.

Finally, unable to stand another second, she squirmed under his touch. "Come to me. I can't bear... You have to...oh!" She gasped as ecstasy drew nearer.

A shudder ran through his long, masculine frame as he lifted himself on his arms. With his gaze burning into hers, he slid along her body until he was in position. He came smoothly and easily into her, filling an emptiness she hadn't known she had.

When they were fully melded, he held her close, one hand tangled in her hair. "I think this was always meant to be," he said, a raw huskiness in his voice, as if it hurt to speak.

"I know." She smoothed the hair from his forehead. "I always wondered...."

He understood. "We both did. That night...I've never forgotten how you felt, how sweet your kisses were. How sweet they are now..."

Tears rushed to her eyes, and she was filled with the terrible poignancy of lost dreams and foolish hopes and all those things she'd felt in his arms so long ago.

"Don't," she whispered. "I don't want to remember *then.* There's only now."

She writhed against him, pressing upward, meeting his thrusts with increasing pleasure. He moved quicker, and she sensed that he was no longer holding a part of himself back.

Neither was she. The red haze of need blotted out reality and there was only the magic of his arms, the wildness of his kisses and the rapture that grew and grew.

"Oh. Oh. Oh," she whispered fiercely.

Seth felt the ripples of her climax, a molten pool of lava closing around him. His hold on his own hunger collapsed and he thrust deeply, rapidly into those heated depths while wave after wave of bliss rolled through him like thunder across the mountain peaks above the valley.

At last, spent, he lay in her arms. With the little strength that remained, he turned them to the side so that she didn't have to bear the brunt of his weight.

Her hands fluttered over his shoulders and into his hair. He heard the little crooning noises she made. There was happiness in the sound, and he felt suddenly humble.

And utterly content.

Alarm flickered along his nerve endings, rising from that lonely, soulless place that remained within him no matter how hard he tried to stamp it out.

Danger, it whispered urgently. *Danger.*

Some part of him knew that here in her arms he'd gone too far, too deep, during this encounter, that she was now too much a part of him.

He quickly denied it. This was sex, plain and simple. He'd played fair. He'd told her there were no strings, no promises, no future. He'd been honest with her.

An unexpected ache settled under his breastbone, harsh, stabbing thrusts of yearning unconnected to physical need. He couldn't figure out where it came from, or why. Inside, he felt torn by conflicts he couldn't define.

She stirred in his arms, then kissed his chin.

Like the sun breaking through a storm, peace flowed into him, its source unknown. No, it was from her, he admitted. She was the source of the confusion, but the contentment also came from her. He'd worry about tomorrow when it came, but not now, not when he held an angel in his arms and stars lay in sparkling drifts around them....

He dosed, then woke with a warm, sensuous feeling. Amelia's eyes were closed, but she moved very slowly, very sexily against him. He realized his body had been awake for some time. He was ready for her again.

''Wait,'' he murmured when she planted a row of flaming kisses along his throat. He replaced the condom with a fresh one. There was no point in taking unnecessary chances, even though, he realized, part of him didn't give a damn about the consequences of making love with this woman.

They made love again, more leisurely this time but with no less pleasure.

''Was it what you thought it would be all those years ago?'' he asked as they rested again.

''More,'' she avowed. ''More than my wildest dreams.'' She opened her eyes. A light seemed to glow from inside her as she confided, ''And I had some pretty wild ones about us for years after that night.''

He was more than gratified by her answer. It reached right down into him and soothed some hurt he hadn't known he had. He knew he had to give something back. "Me, too," he admitted. "My fantasies were never about movie stars. They were all of you."

Her smile was sweet and somehow vulnerable, the way it had been seventeen years ago. But there was no way to recapture the past or the innocence of that one enchanted night. He felt the familiar bitterness of regret mix with the old memories. "We were too young."

"Are we old enough now?" she questioned.

He shrugged. "Holding you, I feel like that seventeen-year-old again, wanting, but knowing it can never be."

She moved away from him, pushing the pillow behind her as she leaned against the headboard. "Why?"

He had to be truthful. "I'm not a marrying man." He looked at the clock. "It's time to get ready for the wedding."

Those two sentences, following one upon the other, were so incongruous, he would have laughed had the moment not been so fragile.

He rose, pulled on sweats, then laid her clothing, and the cast he could scarcely remember removing, on the bed, then left the room, giving her privacy.

After showering and dressing in a formal suit, he checked the house, which was empty. The bridal party had gone to the church. He went to Amelia's sitting room door. It was open. Entering, he called out, ''Ready?''

''Yes.''

She appeared in a long, finely pleated skirt of dark copper with a floral blouse with coppery tones. Small diamond studs were her only jewelry.

Driving to the country church, he tried to think of something to say, some small talk to ease the tension between them. He opened his mouth.

''Please don't say you're sorry,'' she said before he could speak.

''I won't,'' he answered. ''Whatever else I might be, I'm not sorry for sharing that with you.''

When he glanced her way, she nodded solemnly, as if they'd made a pact. Neither said another word the rest of the way to the church.

Chapter Six

The wedding bothered Seth more than he wanted to admit. Beau and Roni had accepted him as their half brother years ago due to Uncle Nick. When Beau had asked him to be the best man, Seth couldn't refuse.

After seeing Amelia seated next to Alison, he went to the pastor's study to join Beau.

"Glad you're here," Beau said in relief. "Trevor made it, too. He got home last night from Texas."

"Uncle Nick told him he'd better be here or else," Seth said with a smile. "Am I supposed to carry a ring?"

"Oh, yeah. Here it is."

The gold seemed to burn Seth's fingers as he slipped the ring into a pocket of the formal suit.

Beau chuckled. ''Damn, but I'm nervous. I didn't think I would be. Uncle Nick gave me the responsibilities-of-a-husband lecture yesterday.''

''The one about building your marital house big enough to hold your wife and all those she loves, including the children she'll give you?''

''That's the one.''

''I heard him give it to Travis when he and Julie married. I wonder if he changed it any when Travis married Alison,'' Seth said.

The men exchanged solemn smiles.

The minister entered. ''Ready?''

''Ready,'' Beau said. ''What did I do with the ring?'' He checked his pockets.

''You gave it to me. Come on.'' Seth was as anxious to get through the ceremony as the groom. He felt he walked a tightrope between two points of equal peril.

They followed the pastor to the front of the church. Marta was playing soft music on the organ, and as Seth passed, he smiled at her. Working together at the B and B, they'd become fast friends the past couple of weeks. He noticed Miss Pickford and her cousin, Shelby's birth grandmother, were seated with the bride's adopted family, so apparently all was well with them.

Shelby's bridesmaid, a friend from back East, took her place with the wedding party. The bridal march began. The audience rose as Shelby, escorted by her father, came down the aisle looking like an angel.

Beau was obviously transfixed by her beauty. Seth glanced toward Amelia, seated at the end of the Dalton pew. She was standing, too, and he worried about her taxing her ankle.

Her gaze met his briefly, then she looked away, her eyes, usually a cool shade of blue, dark and mysterious with thoughts he couldn't read.

All his life, he'd found most women fairly transparent. They were attracted to the Dalton name and his perceived place as the oldest of his generation. They didn't know his real story. No one did.

Would they still want him if they knew his true past, the harsh reality and grinding poverty of his early years before he became a Dalton? That was easy to answer: no.

He focused on the ceremony as the bride joined Beau and the couple exchanged vows. When it was time, he handed over the ring. The bridesmaid did the same. The minister pronounced them man and wife.

This time the couple led the way down the aisle. Seth stole a glance at Amelia as he and the bridesmaid followed.

She was observing the flowers at the side of the dais, her mind obviously far away. He'd never seen her look so pensive, so lost in a place where only she could go.

When she met his eyes, she smiled in that way she had, with the part of herself that she showed the public. Like him, she had her secrets. Like him, she'd been hurt by those who were supposed to watch over her.

Luck had been with both of them. She'd had her grandparents, and he'd had Uncle Nick.

After the wedding, Seth saw the parents and wedding party off, then returned for Amelia and drove them into town.

The reception was at the community center in order to accommodate the many friends who had known the Dalton gang all their lives. After the opening waltzes, Zack dedicated the next song to Uncle Nick. Everyone roared as "Another One Bites the Dust" boomed over the speakers.

Beau cracked up. Still grinning, he pointed to Seth. Zack did, too. Seth gave them a glare that was more real than either of them knew. He was aware of several people glancing from him to Amelia. The last thing he wanted was gossip that might hurt her.

His duty dances done, he joined Amelia at the festive table decorated with fall blooms. His relatives were taking it for granted that they were a couple. Until her ankle healed, he supposed they were.

"We've never danced," he said, realizing it was true.

"And probably never will." She gave him a sardonic grin that did funny things to his insides.

He responded to the implied challenge. "Oh, yes," he murmured, "we surely will. After all, there are two more Daltons to be married off."

"Three," she corrected.

He shook his head. "Trevor and Roni, not me."

She shot him a speculative glance. "Why not?"

"It isn't in the cards."

The bleakness of the years ahead hit him with the suddenness of a sucker punch. He remembered Uncle Nick's grief over his wife and child, and the twin brothers he'd lost the year before that. Yet his heart had been big enough to include the orphans in his loving kindness through it all.

That was the man Seth wished his father had been, that he himself longed to be. Listening to the laughter and joking advice directed at the bridal pair, he frowned as he tried to figure out what was bugging him today.

Trevor settled in the chair on the other side of Amelia. "How's the ankle?" he asked.

"It's much better," she said in her stoic way. "How're your ribs? I heard you cracked a couple."

Trevor rubbed a spot on his lower rib cage. "Yeah. Pretty stupid of me. Luckily, I heal fast."

"How come you were riding bulls?" Seth asked. "I thought you stuck with roping and the easy stuff."

His cousin, usually a smart mouth with a teasing, good-natured manner, shrugged. "Like I said, it was stupid."

Seth saw Amelia's concerned glance at the younger man and knew she, too, had caught the subtle undercurrent of bitterness in his tone. Something had happened to Trevor, the lighthearted, on the trip. Seth was willing to bet that "something" had been a female.

So what else was new? Men had been falling for pretty faces since the beginning of time.

The attempt at cynicism was feeble. Mostly Seth felt a surge of sympathy for the other man.

Veronica, who answered only to her nickname, Roni, brought two plates over and placed one in front of Amelia. ''Here. These guys will let you starve before they think of feeding you.''

Seth rose. ''I'll get the drinks.''

After grabbing glasses of champagne for everyone, he and Trevor loaded plates for themselves and returned to the women.

''Here's to love and marriage and all that,'' Roni said brightly, raising the crystal flute.

''Yeah,'' Trevor agreed, his smile not at all sincere.

Seth lifted his glass. A tremor from that secret, troubled place shook him as he raised his own glass for the toast.

Amelia, he noted, barely let the champagne touch her lips. Her eyes were fathoms deep as she glanced at him, then looked away and raised the glass once more, this time taking a larger swallow.

Bitterness rushed upward, engulfing him. Riding on its crest were all the things he'd once hoped for—a real family, a safe place to come home to, someone to care about whether he was a good person or not.

Finally his luck had changed. In Lost Valley he'd found everything his young heart desired. For years, it had been enough.

At seventeen, he'd discovered things that boy

hadn't known about—the sweetness of passion, the drive to mate, the need to share that basic human instinct, not with just anyone, but with *the* one....

Because of a past he could deny but never erase, those were things beyond his reach. He'd always known that.

His gaze was drawn to Amelia. Drinking in her quiet, vibrant beauty, he wished life could be different.

When the bride and groom finally left amid a shower of birdseed and good wishes, he held out a hand. "Come on, Red. It's time to go home."

At Roni's interested perusal, he realized how intimate that had sounded.

"I'll see you two at the ranch," he added, committing himself to leaving the B and B. "Tomorrow," he said, qualifying the statement.

At the B and B, Amelia thanked Seth for taking her to the wedding. "I'm beginning to feel like cargo, hauled around from place to place," she admitted with a little laugh that she thought didn't sound at all forced.

"I can imagine." He turned on the gas fire in her sitting room. "Need anything?"

"No, thank you. Uh, thanks for your help. Marta and I can handle breakfast for Shelby's folks in the morning, so you can enjoy being with your family without a trace of guilt." She'd prepared this speech on the way home and thought it sounded confident and sincere.

''Throwing me out?'' he asked, a smile kicking up the corners of his mouth. ''I'm staying here for the night. After breakfast, I thought we could both go to the ranch for a visit.''

There was no need to make a habit of hanging around the Daltons. ''I have things to do here, but thanks for thinking of me,'' she told him.

He frowned. ''What happened today is going to make things awkward for us, isn't it?''

While he thrust his hands in his pockets and paced the carpet, she considered and discarded several replies.

''You don't have to worry. It won't happen again,'' he said, coming to a halt in front of her.

Her disappointment was so keen that she stared at her lap so he wouldn't see it in her eyes. He dropped to his haunches, touched her cheek, then lifted her chin.

''Not because it wasn't great,'' he said softly, regretfully, ''but because it has no place to go.''

She moved away from his touch. ''Such as a wedding?'' she asked playfully, determined to give nothing of her inner feelings away. ''I knew that. Neither of us wants a deep involvement, so let's call it a day and—and just be friends.''

He was silent so long she thought he wasn't going to answer. ''Right,'' he finally said. ''Friends. If that's possible after this afternoon.''

''It is,'' she assured him coolly, stubbornly. ''It's a case of mind over…'' She realized where that train of thought was going.

"Over passion?"

She shrugged. "Something like that."

He gazed into her eyes another long second, then headed for the door. "There are a million reasons to stay away from each other, but will they be enough?"

Without waiting for a reply, he left. She listened to his footsteps in the hallway. A little later, she heard him again, this time in the great room. Then the flames in the grate flickered as the front door opened and closed. A car engine started a minute later.

He was gone.

After a bit, she rose and hobbled to the sitting room door and closed it. From out front, she heard the return of Shelby's family. She only had to get through the next morning, and they, too, would be gone. Then she would have two weeks to herself to rest. She felt as if she needed the time to recover from a long, debilitating illness.

Her grandmother had once told her she was "heartsick" after Amelia's parents divorced.

Amelia knew the feeling. She'd loved Seth Dalton seventeen years ago with all the foolish, yearning wonder of first love. Upon leaving, she'd felt sick inside, too.

The following week Amelia found she could accomplish the chores quite competently by pacing herself. She worked for an hour or so, then sat with her foot propped up for at least twenty minutes. If she detected any swelling, she used cold compresses to relieve it. Aspirin took care of any discomfort at night. The next Monday, a gray, sullen day of clouds and an intermittent wind, she went to the clinic.

"Everything is looking great," Beau told her, studying an X ray of her ankle. "You don't need the support of the cast anymore, but you do need to start an exercise program to regain full mobility of the foot."

He gave her an illustrated brochure and a stretchy band, then Shelby helped her go through each motion so she knew how to perform it correctly. Marta drove her home, then went to the grocery for milk and fresh produce.

"Are you sure you'll be okay?" the cook asked upon returning. "Snow is predicted for tonight and tomorrow."

"I'm sure. I don't have a thing to do, except eat, sleep and catch up on my reading. You run home to your family before they start worrying about your being caught in the storm."

Alone that evening, Amelia read the novel she'd started a month ago. So much had happened since the night Seth had appeared at her door and found the B and B full. With hindsight, she acknowledged that she should have sent him on his way.

Suddenly a siren rent the perfect stillness of the night. Amelia listened, expecting the sound to fade as the ambulance headed toward the hospital at the county seat, or perhaps south to Boise, if more extensive medical care was needed.

The sound stopped abruptly.

Glancing out the window, she saw the gentle sifting of snow over the lighted path. The storm had already laid an inch of white fluff over the landscape. That could be bad for the patient in the ambulance.

However, she could be reading too much into the situation. Perhaps the siren was a portend of joy, announcing that a child was about to be born, the mother taken to Beau's clinic for the birth.

Laying a hand over her abdomen, Amelia wondered how it felt to carry a baby, to deliver it with its father standing by to lend support. She'd seen a birth on TV, but that had been like watching one of those educational films they'd had in high school, not quite real, as if the whole thing was being staged for the camera.

Before she could stop it, an image of Seth came to mind, caring for her after she was hurt. Seth, tender and considerate. A little bossy, but in a nice way.

A sigh escaped her. She finished the novel and put it in the bookcase under the window.

In her pleasant bedroom, she turned the light out and snuggled down into the pillow. Listening to the wind pick up outside, she was glad she didn't have to go out. She was equally glad she and Seth hadn't made love in here, so there were no memories associated with him in her bed.

Only in a thousand other places in her imagination, a part of her mockingly suggested.

She'd managed to shut him out of her thoughts during the past week…well, some of the time. She closed her eyes and hoped sleep would come soon.

Amelia woke with a start. Alert, her heart pounding, she listened. Hearing nothing, she decided she must have been having a bad dream. At that moment, the doorbell rang, then someone knocked and called her name.

"Seth?" she murmured, not sure if she was still dreaming.

"Amelia?"

Climbing out of bed, she grimaced as she put her weight on her tender ankle and slipped into the fuzzy scuffs. She hurried down the hall to the front door, putting on the robe as she went. A sense of déjà vu swept over her as she observed the person standing outside the door.

"What is it?" she asked as soon as she had the door open. "What's wrong?"

He swept a dark felt Stetson off and swatted it against his leg to dislodge the clinging snow, then came inside. With the door closed and locked, he turned to her. "It's Uncle Nick. He had another heart attack last night."

"Oh, no! How is he?"

"Stable, Beau says."

"He's at the clinic?"

"Yeah. There wasn't time to get him to Boise. A clot had formed in a major artery. Beau used a new anticoagulant medicine on him. It worked like a charm.''

''I heard the ambulance. I wondered who was hurt.''

''That was someone else—a woman having a baby. The paramedics had to deliver it. The new mother and baby are at the clinic, too, along with the husband and Ruth. It was a full house.'' He smiled wryly.

Ruth was a licensed midwife and also worked as Beau's nurse in the clinic. Her sister-in-law was the clinic receptionist. Their husbands, who were brothers, owned the local hardware store.

Intertwined lives, Amelia reflected. Typical of a small town, and comforting, too. There were always others to care and to help out in an emergency.

She helped Seth remove his jacket, then hung it on a peg. He sat on the bench of the hall tree and tugged off his boots. ''Forgot my gloves,'' he said, rubbing his hands together. ''I left the city in a hurry when Zack called.''

''Come on. I'll fix some hot chocolate. Or would you prefer coffee?''

''Coffee, please.''

She ushered him to her sitting room, turned on the gas logs, then hurried to the kitchen. The clock indicated it was a couple of minutes before five. Nearly time to get up, so she might as well start the day early, she decided. She'd never get back to sleep at this late hour.

After preparing omelettes for two, she fixed toast

and muffins along with glasses of milk and mugs of fresh coffee, and placed the food on a tray for each of them.

Making two trips, she served him, then settled in the rocking chair with the second tray across her lap. "When did your uncle have the heart attack?"

"A little after ten last evening. He and Trev were watching a nature show when Uncle Nick grabbed his chest, said he was having pain, then passed out. Zack and Honey had gone to bed. Trev woke them, also Travis and Alison, then called Beau. Beau said to bring him to the clinic pronto. They did. Zack called me from there. I picked up Roni and broke land speed records getting here."

"So all of you were at the clinic the rest of the night?"

"Right. Roni is staying with Uncle Nick while the rest of us get some sleep. With the whole family there and the beds filled, I said I'd come over here."

"I'm glad you did," Amelia said sympathetically. "You and your family are welcome anytime you need a place to crash."

"Thanks."

His quiet murmur of gratitude did things to her heart. The worry over his uncle was evident in the darkness of his eyes and the lines etched on his brow. Seth was a man of compassion and deep family loyalty.

"Your uncle is lucky to have you," she said. "All of you. I remember in school how you looked after the younger ones. On the school bus, it was understood that Roni always had a place next to you if she wanted it."

"She was so young when her dad—our dad—" he corrected, "died. When she started school, she was scared. I knew what fear was like—"

He stopped abruptly, looking chagrined at disclosing this much about himself. Amelia knew Roni's mother had died from a hemorrhage during a miscarriage when the girl was around two years old. By one of those ironies of fate, Seth's mother had been hired to care for Roni and Beau during a rodeo the brothers had entered. That's how she and Seth had come to live with them.

"I remember how difficult it was to change schools so often," she told him. "After a while, I just didn't think about it anymore. Children adjust."

"They have to in order to survive," he said, an undercurrent of anger, perhaps despair, in his tone.

She wondered what memories he harbored from his childhood, what his life had been like. His mother had worked at various jobs and seemingly moved around a lot—Texas, Oklahoma, New Mexico.

Amelia wondered why, but now wasn't the time to ask.

Seeing that he'd finished his meal, she quickly did the same, knowing he needed to get some rest. "The single room is ready if you would like to go to bed. I'll wake you if anyone calls."

"Good." He rose, then hesitated. "I appreciate your help," he said a bit stiffly.

She smiled. "That's what friends are for, right?"

"Right."

He insisted on carrying the trays to the kitchen. After he left, she dressed and straightened up her quarters, then watered the house plants and generally busied herself for the rest of the morning. At noon, she ate a sandwich and settled on the sofa to rest her right foot.

Her thoughts, no longer occupied with mundane chores, immediately went to the man who slept in the small bedroom on the east side of the house. She pondered the birth of the baby and the near death of the old man.

Birth and death. The cycle of life. And between those two extremes were all the joy and misery inherent in the human condition.

Smiling at this bit of melodrama, she stretched out and pulled the afghan over her legs, but her mind wouldn't give her rest. For years she hadn't thought about anything but making the B and B a success. Since the incident of hurting her ankle and falling on Seth in one fell swoop, as it were, she was filled with all the hazy, intense yearnings of her uncertain youth.

She was sure the same was true for Seth.

Her heart set up an awful clamor, and she had to press a hand to her chest to hold in the ache. What was it from his past that had convinced him he could never have a lasting relationship?

The alleged male fear of commitment?

That didn't make sense. Everything about him indicated a deep, caring nature.

What secrets from his youth had scarred him so that he refused to contemplate sharing his life?

Unlike her, he hadn't married in a heady whirl of excitement, and learned to regret that hasty act. He might have loved someone, though, and lost her to another.

Amelia couldn't imagine a woman not loving Seth in return if he loved her. Knowing the answers to the haunting questions lived in his past, she forced her mind to think of practical matters. The day would be busy.

She dozed off, then was awakened by her name being called. ''In here,'' she said.

Seth appeared, looking refreshed after six hours of sleep and a shower. He was dressed in jeans and a Western-style shirt with a black leather vest. He entered the room soundlessly in thick winter socks.

''I'm heading for the clinic,'' he told her. ''I don't know what time I'll be back.''

''Wait. I have a box of muffins for you to take over in case anyone wants a snack.'' She led the way to the kitchen and handed him the treat she'd packed earlier. ''Here's a key to the side door next to your room. You may as well keep it while you're here.''

He put the key on the ring with his others and surprised her with a wry grin. ''Does this mean I won't have to keep waking you up in the middle of the night?''

''Exactly,'' she said. ''Why don't all of you come over for dinner tonight? I was planning on cooking a ham, anyway, so there'll be plenty for everyone.''

He nodded. ''I'll call if there's a change in plans.''

She walked him to the door. He pulled on his boots and stood, paused, then brushed a brief—too brief!—kiss over her lips.

''Thanks for everything,'' he said huskily, and was gone.

Peering out, she saw the snow was still falling, but the flakes were smaller and not so heavy as during the night. The pristine blanket of white covered everything in sight, including Seth's truck. She watched while he cleaned the windshield, then cranked up the engine, vapor from the tailpipe frosting the air as he backed out and headed across town to the clinic.

A glow warmed her from the inside out. She was glad he'd come to her place when he'd needed to rest. She'd always thought of the old house as a sanctuary, but now she realized it had been so because of those in it, because they had loved her just as she loved them.

Just as she loved Seth Dalton.

Chapter Seven

"The question is—who will stay with Uncle Nick?" Zack, still in his lawman's uniform, asked, his manner worried. "He's insisting on returning to the ranch."

Amelia listened in sympathy to the conversation among the Daltons that evening. They were all at the B and B for dinner, while Ruth, the midwife-nurse, stayed at the clinic with the patients.

"He shouldn't be alone," Beau told them, speaking with a doctor's voice of authority. "Especially at the ranch. It's too far out of town. With the twins working the fall roundup and the rest of us with job obligations, we'll have to find someone to live in or to drive out each day."

Amelia glanced over the group. The twins worked long hours on the ranch at this time of the year. Zack had to patrol the whole county as part of his job and often worked double shifts. Beau had the medical clinic. Zack's wife ran a dance school, Travis's taught business classes at the high school up in Council, while Beau's new bride, Shelby, was a nurse. Their time was filled.

''Who can we get?'' Zack asked in a dismal tone. ''The ranch is nearly an hour from town, a long drive each way, not to mention possible rain and snow and all that. The women around here who don't have outside jobs already have families to take care of.''

Beau nodded. ''Maybe someone from Boise?''

''Huh.'' Zack's skeptical grunt showed what he thought of that idea.

''Surely we can find a person on a temporary basis,'' Roni said. ''It's fall. With all the holidays coming up, someone must need to make extra money.''

Dead silence ensued.

Roni, looking tired, pale and worried, finally murmured, ''I have a big presentation this Friday, but I can take next week off. Can Uncle Nick stay at the clinic until Saturday?''

Everyone looked at the doctor.

''Not in the clinic emergency room. We need the space.'' Beau thought it over. ''Shelby and I can put him upstairs in our bedroom, or maybe in the cottage with a monitor.''

"Uncle Nick won't tolerate being monitored like a baby," Trevor said, speaking up for the first time. "I know I wouldn't like it."

"So what's another idea?" Roni asked.

No one had any.

Hesitantly, Amelia cleared her throat. "Uh, this is a pretty slow time of the year for me. In fact, I don't have anyone coming in until Saturday morning, and then it's only a family and one other couple for the night. There's plenty of room for your uncle." She glanced at Zack. "You could bring him to town each morning, if you like, and take him home each evening. He certainly wouldn't be in the way."

A moment of silence passed. Amelia wondered if maybe she shouldn't have butted in. It wasn't her concern.

"That's an idea," Seth said, approval in his voice.

Relief washed over her.

"I think so, too," Beau agreed. "He could stay the night as well, couldn't he? That way, he'd be close to the clinic in case he has another spell. I'd like to keep an eye on him for the next week or ten days."

Seth speared Amelia with a keen gaze. "Would that be too hard on you?"

"Not at all." She felt somewhat flustered as he continued to stare at her intently. "He can stay in Zack's old room, the one across the hall from your...from the single room,'' she corrected. After all, Seth was hardly a permanent guest.

''I'll be in the carriage house with my classes during the day,'' Honey reminded them. ''I can help keep an eye on Uncle Nick. Amelia and I can tie him down if he gets too cantankerous or tries to make a break for the ranch.''

That brought laughter and broke the tension in the room. Amelia went to the kitchen for the dessert she'd made that afternoon. Seth followed.

''You don't have to do this,'' he said, taking the tray holding banana pudding, spoons and bowls from her.

''It won't be any trouble.''

His laughter surprised her. ''Then you don't know Uncle Nick,'' he advised. ''I'll come up tomorrow night after work. Since I'd planned to be in the Lost Valley office on Thursdays and Fridays anyway, then at the ranch on the weekends, this will work out fine. I can move the schedule up a week. I'll need the single room.''

She nodded. ''I'll save it for you.''

''Or I could share yours if you have a full house.''

Her gaze flew to his.

''Just joking.'' He grinned, but his eyes didn't hide the hot flames of desire that blazed in him.

Like the earth-shaking eruption from a volcano, heat poured through her, an inferno of need and longing so strong she had to look away before he saw it.

''There's ice cream in the freezer,'' she quickly said. ''I'll bring it in case anyone wants some.''

''Sorry, I shouldn't have said that,'' he murmured in a husky tone that only increased the turmoil inside her.

She nodded. ''That's okay. We're friends, remember? Friends can say things to each other.''

He hesitated, his eyes still on her, then nodded and headed for the great room.

By nine, the Daltons, having had little sleep the past twenty-four hours, had gone their various ways. It had been decided that Beau would bring their uncle over the next morning, which would be Wednesday. If he did well, they would let the older man return to the ranch the following Wednesday. If they could keep him away that long.

On Wednesday morning Seth picked up Roni at the cottage behind the medical clinic. The sun wasn't up, but the sky was slowly turning from black to opalescent gray with a few pink streamers fluttering at the horizon like forgotten bunting left over from a party.

His half sister covered a yawn, then looked back at the sleepy town before they drove over the ridge and out of sight. ''I worry about leaving,'' she said. ''I feel guilty.''

Seth knew the feeling.

She sighed and faced forward. ''I've taken Uncle Nick for granted. He's always been there for us, but now, when he's in need, we're leaving. It's like our jobs are more important than he is."

"He'll be well cared for," Seth reminded her. "Beau will take him over to the B and B this morning. Amelia will keep an eye on him."

As he mentioned her name, heat flushed through him like water through a hot radiator. He'd tried a hundred times to explain that afternoon of lovemaking to himself, but to no avail. Worse, that old saying was true: once was not enough.

Roni smiled. "Poor Amelia."

"I don't think Uncle Nick will intimidate her," Seth said dryly. "She can hold her own."

Roni kicked off her shoes and propped her feet on the dash. "Amelia is nice, but she isn't family." She hesitated, then said, "Unless you're planning on making her a Dalton?"

Seth shot his younger sibling a warning glance.

"You needn't look daggers at me," she scolded. "It's apparent to everyone that there's something between you and Amelia. Admit it."

"She's an attractive woman," he said grudgingly.

"So there is something." Roni sighed. "You'll move back to Lost Valley and I'll be alone in Boise."

"I'm still keeping office hours in the city."

"For how long?" she asked forlornly.

Seth shrugged. "For the foreseeable future." He gave Roni a speculative glance. "Aren't there any men in your life? What's wrong with the guys at your company?"

She snorted. ''Not my type.''

''You don't like old, beer-bellied, cigar-smoking geezers?'' he inquired, as if vaguely shocked. They laughed, then were quiet for a few moments before he asked, ''Seriously, haven't you found anyone who stirred your insides, made your knees go weak and all that?''

''Is that what happened to you?''

''Don't try to change the subject. Uncle Nick will be after you before too long. Do you have a sad tale of a broken heart to explain your lack of a mate?''

''Nothing so dramatic.''

''There was someone,'' Seth concluded.

''The least likely person you would ever imagine,'' she said lightly. ''Think of the first man.''

It took him a few seconds to figure it out. ''Adam. As in Honey's brother, Adam Smith? I didn't realize there was anything between you two. You've been in contact with him since Honey and Zack married?''

''No, we haven't been in contact. He made it clear at the wedding he wasn't interested, so no, there isn't anything between us.''

A month ago, Seth would have dropped the subject, but now he found he was intensely interested in matters of the heart. ''That's tough,'' he said sympathetically.

''What about you and Amelia?'' Roni asked.

He hesitated a fraction too long.

''So I was right. You two have a thing going.''

''No,'' he stated. ''As you said, she's nice. And

smart. Too smart to get involved with a Dalton.'' His brief laughter sounded hollow even to his ears.

''I'm sorry,'' Roni said softly.

''For what?''

''That she doesn't love you, too.''

Seth controlled with an effort the wild flow of emotion that sent electrical currents to all parts of his body. ''You're jumping to conclusions, little sis. I'm not in love and never plan to be.''

''Because of what happened between our father and your mother?'' she asked.

For an instant, he wanted to tell her the truth, to shed the lies that hovered around him like a black miasma. He stared at the road. It seemed to stretch out forever, an empty path heading toward nothing except a blank horizon.

''Seth?'' Roni said, sounding worried.

''Something like that,'' he finally replied.

Instead of grouchy, Amelia found Nicholas Dalton to be charming and in good spirits.

''It's mighty nice of you to put me up,'' he told her when he and Beau arrived at noon on the dot. He swept his hat off. ''Beau, where're those flowers?''

Beau handed his uncle a bouquet. Uncle Nick presented them to Amelia. The pale yellow roses were blushed with pink at the outer edges of the petals.

''Oh, you shouldn't have,'' she said. ''But I'm glad you did. These are perfectly lovely. Thank you so much.''

''My pleasure.''

Uncle Nick beamed at her, his blue-as-the-sky eyes so gleeful, she became a little worried. The Dalton patriarch was known for his plotting ways. What was he thinking?

''Uh, I'll put these in water.'' She hurried to the kitchen to do so.

''Seth here?'' he asked, following at her heels.

''No, he and Roni had to return to the city, but he'll be here tonight, he said, as soon as he clears up, quote—a mountain of paperwork—unquote.''

She clipped the ends of the flower stalks, added two aspirins and a spoonful of sugar to the water to preserve and feed the plants, then returned to the great room and placed the vase on the buffet table.

''The boy works too hard, always has,'' his uncle declared. ''Well, where do you want these old bones?''

''Uh, the bedroom is down this way.''

She led him to the large guest room across the hall from Seth's room. Beau was already there with his uncle's luggage.

''You have a sink in the room,'' the nephew said, pointing out the amenities. ''The full bath is across the hall and down a bit, next to the room where Seth will be.''

The older man glanced around. ''This is nice.''

''There's a television in the great room.'' Amelia thought of the stiff Victorian sofa and divan. ''And also in my sitting room. It's more comfortable in there…and cheaper to heat,'' she added, realizing the older man might need a reason to enter her private space.

"Good thinking," he said approvingly.

She led the way to her sitting room. The gas logs blazed merrily, two violets were in bloom and the afghan tossed over the sofa invited one to stretch out and nap. Once Uncle Nick was settled on the sofa with the remote control device at hand and a news show on the TV, Amelia walked Beau to the front door.

"Anything I need to know about his care?" she asked.

"I fixed a pill box with the medication he's to take each day. I left it on the vanity in his room. Keep an eye on that, but don't make a fuss about it. I want him to take responsibility for himself. That's important for someone his age. It helps keep him alert."

"Right."

After the doctor returned to his office, Amelia went to the sitting room to ask her guest if he'd had lunch. She found him already asleep. Covering him with the afghan, she wondered what Seth would look like when he was seventy. His uncle was still a handsome man, spry and lean.

Uncle Nick didn't smoke, wasn't overweight and led an active life, but this was his second heart attack. He'd had the first one in early spring.

Worry gnawed at her. Did heart trouble run in the family? Would Seth share the same fate?

Realizing where this was leading, she forced herself to return to mundane matters, such as lunch for herself.

After eating, she brought all her accounts and tax records up to date, then made a cup of tea and returned to the sitting room. Her guest had removed his shoes and was now lying prone on the sofa, sound asleep. The TV picture was on, but the sound had been muted. She turned the television off.

Sitting in the rocker and propping her feet on the ottoman, she sipped the tea and watched the clouds grow thin and dissipate. Seth should have a full moon for his return trip that evening. Assuming he made it. He might stay in the city and drive up in the morning.

Sighing, she closed her eyes and let herself drift into sleep. An hour later, a breath of cool air woke her.

She heard footsteps coming quietly along the hall. Her heart started a tom-tom beat, recognizing the footfalls before her conscious mind did.

Seth appeared at the door. His dark eyes flicked over her and the older man and a pleased smile appeared on his handsome face.

Uncle Nick shifted, opened his eyes and sat up.

''Well,'' Seth drawled, ''I turn my back for a minute and then find you sleeping with the best-looking female in town,'' he accused his relative.

''Darn right,'' Uncle Nick said, chuckling. ''I know a good thing when I see it.''

The dark eyes turned her way. ''Yeah, so do I.''

Amelia suppressed a tremor of delight at the teasing, sexy perusal. "You men will give me a swelled head," she warned. "My grandpa said that was bad in a person."

"He was a wise man." Uncle Nick frowned at Seth. "Did you get that mountain of work done, or did you skip out early?"

"I skipped, but I brought the work with me. I'll burn the midnight oil," he promised, lifting the portable computer case in his hand.

"Seth is a hard worker," Uncle Nick told Amelia. "All my boys are."

The older man's pride and affection brought the sting of tears to her eyes. Her grandparents had been the same with her. They had encouraged good traits with frequent and lavish praise.

Determined to follow their example rather than that of her impulsive, tempestuous parents, she'd tried to live up to their faith in her. Other than that one stupid act when she was twenty, which she found incomprehensible now, she had lived a frugal, careful life.

Glancing at Seth, she was reminded of that haunting night so long ago when he'd walked her home from a dance she hadn't wanted to attend, and of the passionate interlude in his arms the day of the wedding. Maybe she had more of her parents in her than she'd previously thought.

Hearing the clock chime in the great room, she realized it was time for the evening meal, and stood, forcing away the unexplained bleakness she felt while she excused herself.

In the kitchen, she checked the bean-and-ham casserole simmering in a pot, then prepared salad greens and buttered slices of sourdough bread. Honey popped in to see how things were going. Amelia invited her and Zack over for the meal.

When Shelby called, also to see how things were going, Amelia told her to bring Beau and their son and join them.

It was seven when everyone arrived. Seth helped Amelia serve the dinner. She noted his gaze was often on her.

"What?" she finally asked.

"You're still limping. Are you doing the exercises the way you're supposed to?"

Heat crept up her neck. "Well, uh, some."

Actually, she'd meant to do them, but with everything going on, she tended to forget. She hadn't tried them at all the past three days.

"Yeah, right."

His tone carried a warning. She figured she was in for a lecture, but he said nothing more.

After the simple repast, they returned to the sitting room. Amelia offered tea, wine or decaffeinated coffee.

"How did it go in court today?" Beau asked Seth.

Seth rolled his eyes. "Don't ask. I'm thinking of refusing any more divorce cases."

"A battle, huh?"

"And then some. The couple's four kids told the judge they didn't want a divorce and that he should make the parents attend counseling for a year. The couple banded together and told the kids to mind their own business. The whole bunch ended up crying.''

''What did the judge do?'' Honey asked.

Seth grinned. ''He ordered the family into counseling and told them to report back to him every month. He's going to review the counselor's notes, too, so if they aren't making progress, he'll know about it. He said if they didn't go, he would hold the parents in contempt and make them work in a homeless shelter every weekend for six months so they would learn the value of home and family.''

''A wise man,'' Uncle Nick murmured. ''Divorce is too easy these days. Folks have a tiff and next thing you know, they're splitting up instead of working things out so the family can stay together.''

''Sometimes, if a man beats his family, it's best to part,'' Seth said.

''Women can be abusive, too,'' Honey stated.

Amelia surmised she was thinking of her aunt, who had taken in Honey and her brother, but hadn't wanted them.

Seth conceded this was true, but added, ''Ninety percent of physical abuse cases are caused by men.''

Something in his tone brought a pang to Amelia's heart. She thought of her own parents, with their constant spats and jealous scenes. Now in their late fifties, they were still together, although divorced, and they still quarreled over every tiny thing. She smiled at the absurdity of it all.

At nine o'clock, the other couples said good-night

and Uncle Nick went to his room. After making sure the older man was comfortable, Seth returned to the sitting room. Amelia looked up from the magazine she hadn't yet read.

He sighed as he settled on the sofa, kicked off his shoes and propped his feet up. ''You were smiling earlier when we discussed the divorce case. Care to share?''

Laughing in wry amusement, she explained about her parents, their divorce, the reconciliation. ''All these years I've worried about them. Tonight it finally occurred to me that fighting and making up was their way of getting along. They probably wouldn't enjoy the relationship nearly as much if counseling put an end to the turbulence.''

''A wise conclusion,'' he told her. ''If it works for them…'' He shrugged.

''Yes,'' she agreed. ''But it wouldn't be my way. I want to be like my grandparents. They worked together all their lives and were best friends. They argued once in a while, but mostly they shared things—laughter and sunsets and a sky filled with stars.''

She stopped and swallowed hard as a knot of tears filled her throat.

''You miss them,'' he said gently.

''Sometimes with a dreadful ache,'' she admitted. ''But then I envision them doing something grand, like strolling around heaven and painting the sky in glorious pinks and golds. When I see an especially beautiful sunset, I think of them.''

Gazing into the red-and-yellow flames dancing over the gas logs, she felt as if they flickered in her heart, warm and soothing, and she smiled.

Seth couldn't take his eyes from the woman who sat in a quiet aura of beauty, the fire limning her face in gold and catching the dark glow in her hair. He knew, as if he could see into her heart, the dreams she'd once had, the need inside her for a loving family of her own.

She deserved all those things.

Pain clawed at his gut, reminding him of all the reasons he wasn't, could never be, the man of her dreams.

Why couldn't he have her? some insidious part of him demanded. She wanted him. With her, he would be as honorable as he tried to be for Uncle Nick.

He gritted his teeth as the pain rose, licking fiercely at him as if the fire in the grate had leaped to his soul.

Honorable? he asked himself. When his whole life had never been anything but one big lie?

Amelia had a natural goodness that he could never hope to match. He lived with the knowledge that someday he might be exposed for the impostor he was or that some evil place inside him where even love couldn't reach would manifest itself in the ways of his father. His *real* father, not the ideal one Uncle Nick had given him.

Seth waited out the turmoil and gazed his fill of the beautiful woman who still looked into the fire as if she saw dreams dancing there. Once he'd thought being a Dalton was everything in the world, everything he would ever need, but he'd been a boy at the time.

He hadn't realized the consequences of walking a young girl on the brink of womanhood home from a dance one frosty night. He'd hadn't known the effects of hot kisses and hearts beating wildly together, hadn't known that he would never get over those moments.

The bitter loneliness of childhood, of the years in college and law school proving himself, rose like a choking fog. He hadn't known the past could linger like a hidden devil, waiting for the right time, then laughing in its evil heart as it took the next opportunity to strike, tempting him with the very things he couldn't have—a home, a family, *her*.

"God," he whispered, a prayer, a plea. "Dear God..."

She started as if from sleep, then peered at him. "Did you say something?"

"No," he said, knowing he had to deny the urging of his heart. He shook his head wearily, feeling he'd come through a hard and deadly battle. "Thanks for all your help. I think I'll head off to bed."

She nodded, her expression at once sympathetic. "It's been a long day for you."

He lingered at the door as memories of her sweet passion wafted through him. He had only to take her into his arms and they would both be lost to reason.

"Seth?" she said.

When she caught her bottom lip between her teeth, all the uncertainty that existed between them in her eyes, his determination to be honorable and deal fairly with her was nearly destroyed. Stilling the longing that was stronger than any temptation he'd ever known, he turned away and hurried along the dim hall.

In the dark bedroom, he closed the door and paused, his hand on the knob, and wondered if this was how the original Adam had felt when he was cast out of paradise.

Chapter Eight

Amelia wasn't surprised by the activity at the Dalton homestead on Saturday, but she was a bit intimidated. People were everywhere, milling about, chatting in ever-changing groups in the area between the house, stables and paddocks.

And horses. She hadn't realized the ranch had so many, although she knew from newspapers and ranching magazines that the Seven Devils cutting horses were considered among the best in the West.

A tent similar to the one used for Travis and Alison's wedding reception was set up in the side yard, with tables and folding chairs from the community center inside it.

"A good turnout for the cutting horse sale," Uncle Nick commented as Seth parked near the house. "And a good day for it."

The sky was sunny and the temperature just right for a light jacket or, as so many of the men wore, a long-sleeved shirt and vest with their jeans, boots and Stetsons.

"I haven't seen so many cowboy hats in one place since my grandparents took me to the state fair one year," Amelia said.

She hopped out of the truck and waited as Uncle Nick got out much more slowly than she or Seth. For some reason the older man seemed frail today. Beau had agreed he could come to the stock sale as long as he didn't overtax himself, and provided he went back to the B and B afterward. Seth had promised to see to it. Uncle Nick had winked at Amelia.

Smiling, she wondered if the nephews knew how often their favorite uncle could see right through them and their machinations. She'd found Uncle Nick to be a wonderful companion, full of stories of the early days and the colorful characters who'd come to the valley to make their fortunes. It made her wish she'd lived back then.

"You're to sit on the front porch," Seth said, breaking into her thoughts with his pleasantly deep baritone.

"Yes, Mom," Uncle Nick said meekly.

Amelia laughed. So did the uncle.

"Very funny," Seth muttered, then spoiled it by laughing, too.

When he glanced at her, sensations ran up her

spine and chased down her arms, leaving a trail of gooseflesh. She was glad of her own long-sleeved shirt and nylon jacket.

They escorted his uncle to the porch spanning the front of the original log cabin. He sat in a log chair and soon had a circle of old friends gathered around him as ranchers spotted him and came over to see how he was faring.

''Nothing like the tender care of a good woman to put a man right,'' he declared to one and all, giving Amelia the credit for his good spirits.

She went inside to leave her jacket and speak to the two Dalton women busy in the kitchen. ''How many people do you have at this sale?'' she asked.

Roni answered. ''Zack sent out seventy-five notices, but some ranchers bring their families, so we usually have close to two hundred people.''

''You don't do this every year, do you?''

''No, only when we have horses ready. That's why we send out invitations.''

''I'm excited,'' Honey told Amelia. ''Zack let me help him work with the stock, so I feel that I helped train them. I didn't, of course, but it still makes me proud.''

''Trev told me you two spent more time in the hay than in the paddock,'' Roni said with exaggerated casualness. ''He said no one dared enter the stable without making a lot of noise first.''

''I'll kill him,'' Honey declared, vigorously mixing a huge bowl of pasta salad.

Roni giggled with delight. ''Look, she's blushing.

I didn't think Vegas showgirls were shocked at anything.''

Actually, Honey was a very talented dancer who'd been part of a well-known dance troupe with a Las Vegas contract before she met Zack.

Amelia, well used to the Dalton humor from the years she'd gone to school with them, nudged Honey. ''Ask Roni who got locked in the closet during her senior year in high school while trying to peek through a vent into the boys' locker room.''

''You didn't!'' Honey said, eyes wide as if she was scandalized.

''Well, it was a dare,'' Roni explained, her Dalton-blue eyes sparkling. ''My lookout took off when she saw the custodian coming, and didn't warn me. He proceeded to lock up the place, so I had to yell and ask him to let me out. He took me to the principal and said he'd caught me smoking. Which wasn't true.''

''Yes,'' Amelia, who'd heard the story, agreed, ''but you didn't dispute it because that was better than admitting you were trying to see if the rumors about the Whitaker boy having two—''

The closing of the front door ended the discussion.

''Just when it was getting interesting,'' Honey murmured for their ears alone.

Travis and Alison entered with plastic bags filled with dinner rolls. ''Where do you want these?'' he asked. He placed the rolls where directed, then retreated from the all-female domain.

Amelia emptied jars of three-bean salad into an old-fashioned pickling crock and placed the lid on it. She heaped huge trays to overflowing with barbecued pork, beef and chicken. "Are we taking all this out to the tent?"

Roni shook her head. "We'll have everyone come in here and fix a plate, then they can eat wherever they want."

"About this Whitaker boy," Honey interjected. "Did he have two, uh, whatevers?"

"Well…" Roni drawled dramatically, then grimaced. "Actually I couldn't see the showers."

"You told everyone he did. You collected money from those who made bets with you," Amelia accused.

The youngest Dalton grinned and shrugged. "They should have verified it if they didn't believe me."

Seth came in while they were still laughing. "What's going on in here? We can hear the cackling all the way to the barn."

"Yeah?" Roni challenged. "In that case, there should be fresh eggs for breakfast."

He lofted one dark eyebrow, snagged four beers from a cooler and headed out, muttering about smart-mouthed women.

Amelia, still smiling, helped finish arranging the food and stacks of paper plates and plastic forks. The company of women, she mused. She'd forgotten how much fun something like this could be. She'd loved it when she and her mom and grandmother had worked together while her dad and grandfather did gardening or watched a ball game on TV.

When lunch was ready, Uncle Nick rang a dinner bell mounted on a pole beside the porch, and people flocked in to fill their plates and take them outside to the tables. Amelia and Seth shared a table with Beau and Shelby, who arrived after Saturday morning office hours, along with Nicky, Beau's son from a brief liaison six years earlier.

Life got complicated, she admitted to herself. After her divorce she'd held herself aloof from any entanglements while working in a factory during the day and completing the last two years of her business degree at night. After she'd inherited the Victorian, she'd had all she could do just keeping her chin above the tide of bills, plus expenses for repairing and decorating the B and B.

Listening to Seth and Beau talk about the horses and the auction to come, she felt pity for the animals that had been raised and trained on the ranch and were now to be sold and sent to a new life, far from all that was familiar. Some were sold more than once in their lifetime.

However, she did find the auction fascinating. Zack and the twins put the cutting horses through their paces for the buyers, then the bidding began. Some animals were sold in a group; others were bid on individually and brought prices that opened her eyes to the value of the stock.

As the sky darkened and the air cooled, Seth's

hand closed over hers. ''I think we had better take Uncle Nick home. He's had enough for one day.''

''I was thinking the same,'' Beau said. ''We really appreciate your keeping an eye on him,'' he told Amelia.

''He's no trouble. In fact, I find him quite charming. I'll miss him when he leaves.''

After saying their farewells, they headed for the front porch, where six older men were talking about the horses.

''I think I might be jealous of my uncle,'' Seth murmured as they crossed the lawn. ''He gets to be with you all day. I only get to be with you at night...in my dreams.''

His mouth was smiling as he relayed this information, but his eyes weren't. There was a seriousness in him that bewildered her.

''Don't,'' she said, almost in a whisper. ''Don't tease.''

''I don't think I am.''

''Then don't say it. Unless you mean it.'' She lifted her head and gave him a level stare.

''I thought friends could say anything to each other.''

''There are boundaries. It's better not to cross them.''

Uncle Nick stood. ''I think the bed rest patrol has come for me,'' he joked to his cronies.

''Yeah,'' Seth said in a John Wayne drawl, ''ya coming peacefully or not?''

''Peacefully,'' the old man declared. ''Amelia and

I are going to sit in the back and make out while you drive.''

Seth stepped between the two. ''Like heck,'' he said.

Amid chuckles, the three left.

A smile lingered on her face during the trip to town. At one point her eyes met Seth's in the rear-view mirror. He smiled slightly, but his eyes—oh, heavens, his eyes!

She shivered with delicate apprehension and wondered what those eyes were saying and what this night would bring.

The next morning, Seth showered and pulled on his favorite sweats, along with ''smart'' socks that were supposed to wick moisture away from the feet and keep them warm at any temperature. He made his way down the dim hall to the kitchen.

''I thought I heard you in here. Don't you ever sleep in?'' he asked.

Amelia continued measuring water into a pan of oatmeal. ''Sometimes. Do you always wake up grouchy?''

He paused in the act of filling a mug with coffee. ''I am grouchy, aren't I?''

She gave him one of those if-the-shoe-fits smiles that women were particularly good at. He snorted. ''Since you're so cheerful, you must have slept well,'' he said, his mind not on sleep at all.

''Yes. Did you?''

''No.''

Now she gave him a truly concerned perusal. His heart kicked around a bit. "The bed isn't comfortable?" she asked. "Perhaps I should see about getting a new mattress. That one is seven years old. But the room isn't used very often. The mattress should be—"

"The problem isn't with the bed!" he informed her in a fierce growl that he immediately regretted when her eyes flew open in shock.

Looking away from him, she said in a neutral, very controlled tone, "Then what is it?"

"Me." He sighed, sat on the stool and took a sip of coffee. "You make the best coffee," he muttered, gazing into the mug as if seeking wisdom. "I'm sorry for snapping. I had a restless night."

Her gaze flicked to him, then away.

"Yeah, because of you," he told her, and watched as a delicate shade of pink climbed her neck and settled in her cheeks. "I wanted to come to you, but..."

She stirred the oatmeal as it came to a boil, then turned the burner lower. "But?" she prodded.

"There are complications, Red."

She laughed. "You have a deep, dark past you haven't told anyone about?"

She was joking, but her words stung all the same. "Yeah," he said.

"My grandmother had a saying—tell the truth and thwart the devil. She also said confession was good for the soul."

Amelia's manner invited his confidence if he

wanted to share. He did. He wanted to bare his soul to this woman and have her tell him he hadn't done anything terribly wrong in choosing a new life for himself.

At twelve he hadn't thought it all out in adult terms, but his mom had had no family and he'd known he didn't want to go to his father's only relative—a brother who was as mean and conniving as Seth's old man.

What kid wouldn't choose to be a Dalton and live on a ranch with horses to ride and plenty to eat?

The bitterness that always came when he thought of his past rolled over him, a black fog of despair that nothing could stamp out of his memory. His secrets weren't his alone to share.

He heard sounds in the east wing of the house. "Uncle Nick is up."

She turned off the heat under the oatmeal pan and began sectioning grapefruit. Seth let his gaze drift down her trim figure. Wearing black knit pants and a black-and-white harlequin top, she looked svelte and alluring, but also remote and untouchable.

When she came to the worktable where he sat, he couldn't stop himself from touching. "Amelia," he said, unable to quell the longing.

She looked at him then, really looked at him. "What is it?" she asked, her eyes full of concern.

"This," he muttered, and cupped her face between his hands. He kissed her, knowing he shouldn't, knowing it wasn't fair because there was more between them than a casual satisfying of lust and knowing that he had nothing to give her, nothing worthy of her.

"Mmm," she crooned as the kiss grew passionate.

Her hands swept over his shoulders, touching, caressing, crowding out thought with the growing urgency of desire. He wrapped his arms around her and held her close, tucking her between his thighs as if to totally enclose her within his embrace so that no one—*no one*—could ever take her from him.

"Good morning. Another beautiful day, eh?"

Uncle Nick entered the kitchen, went directly to the cabinet housing the coffee mugs and poured himself a cup.

Seth let Amelia go. Her hands were trembling as she collected bowls from the shelf above the worktable and filled each with fresh fruit. The blush had fled from her face, leaving her pale.

"Sorry," he murmured, angry with himself for putting her in an awkward position.

She nodded without looking at him.

Glancing at his uncle, he saw an approving twinkle in the old man's eyes. Would he be as pleased if he knew that Seth had lied to him all those years ago when he'd claimed not to have any relatives that he knew of?

Seth suddenly remembered his father laughing over cheating another man out of ten dollars during some deal he'd concocted to his benefit.

Like his father, the seeds of deception were sown

deep within him. Seth was as big a con artist as his dad ever was.

"I need some exercise," he said, seized with a need to get out of that sturdy old house with the two finest people he'd ever known watching him with questions in their eyes.

He went to his room, pulled on jogging shoes and a jacket, then took off, the quarreling hounds of guilt and longing chasing him all the way down the pleasant residential streets of Lost Valley and around the lake.

"Let's head over to the resort the boys are building," Uncle Nick suggested after reading the Sunday paper. "It isn't too far to walk."

Amelia stored the paper in a basket in the great room. "I'll get my walking shoes and a jacket."

When she returned, she found her guest at the door, ready to go. She let him set the pace as they crossed the quiet town, went through the community center park and onto the path to the reservoir.

The dam and the small lake that provided the community with water were at the north end of the valley. The resort was less than a quarter mile from the dam. As they approached, they heard the pounding of a hammer.

"I thought he would come here," Uncle Nick murmured, leading the way inside.

Amelia looked around the huge lobby-reception area with interest. The lodge would be a rival to her B and B when it was finished, but other than the rustic cabins and RVs at the fishing resort on the other side of the lake, there were no other places to stay in the area. With the growing number of visitors to the valley, she wasn't awfully worried about business other than the impact during the slow periods.

She patted the massive log supporting huge overhead beams. "Impressive," she said. "It's certainly going to be a solid building."

The hammering stopped. Seth appeared from a room behind the reception area. "Uncle doesn't like log construction."

"We have modern building methods," Uncle Nick said, frowning as he took in the beams and supports. He nodded toward the log beside Amelia. "That one tree could provide enough lumber for a whole house."

"But then the resort wouldn't live up to expectations. People like rustic."

Amelia had never heard Seth sound so cynical. She wondered what had happened since that passionate but tender kiss to make him so aloof and bitter. Was he angry about the passion that existed between them?

It wasn't her fault, she silently protested. It had been there for a long time—years, in fact. Since the night of a dance she'd hadn't wanted to attend. It would have been better if that night had never happened.

Angry for feeling guilty over things she couldn't change, she explored the lodge.

Framing and walls and stairs were in place. One

room was a kitchen. Next to it, with windows that opened onto marvelous views of the lake and the mountains, was the restaurant, she surmised. Other rooms could be used for offices and shops. Walking along a corridor, she peeked into smaller rooms with bathrooms adjoining each. Those were guest rooms.

Going upstairs, she checked out the second story, counting as she did. The lodge would have twenty guest rooms, plus a two-bedroom suite complete with small kitchens, on each end of that floor. She returned to the lobby via stairs at the opposite end of the huge room.

''You could cook a moose in there,'' she said to the men, stopping in front of a stone fireplace.

''Moose stew is going to be a specialty of the house,'' Seth told her, surprising her with the humorous twist.

She smiled at the quip. ''Sounds delicious.''

''But not as good as the fare at your place,'' he added, with an edge to his usually smooth tone.

His uncle nodded approvingly. ''Will the lodge hurt your business?'' he asked her.

She turned away from Seth's dark eyes. ''I don't think so. I know more people would come here for summer recreation if they had a place to stay. A cross-country ski trail around the lake would be a winter draw. The lodge should consider renting skis. With hunting specials in the fall, you should do well.''

''Maybe we should hire you to run the business,'' Seth commented.

She managed a rueful grin. ''No, thanks. I have enough problems keeping up at my place.''

''What about spring?'' his uncle asked. ''What would lure people here in the spring?''

''Wildlife and wildflowers,'' she suggested. ''The county should buy the meadow around the north end of the lake to keep it from being developed. A couple of wildlife blinds in the swampy areas would be great for viewing migrating birds in spring and fall. Lost Valley is on a major flyway.''

''Have you told the county commission these ideas?'' the older man asked.

''It's been mentioned a couple of times,'' she answered.

''Sounds like they need a little prodding.''

Over his shoulder, she saw a smile lift the corners of Seth's mouth. She smiled, too, as they shared the same thought. If Nicholas Dalton decided something should be done, then the commissioners better have a darn good reason why it wasn't.

Seth returned to the city Sunday night. The next two days passed quietly. On Wednesday, Amelia drove her guest to the medical clinic. Beau pronounced him fit enough to return to the ranch. At lunch, Honey volunteered to take him when her classes were over for the day.

''Next week is Thanksgiving,'' Uncle Nick reminded Amelia when he was packed and ready to leave at five that afternoon. ''We'll be cooking at the ranch. Come join us.''

She thanked him, but shook her head. "I'll have guests that weekend."

"For the holiday?" he demanded.

"Yes. Nearly a full house. People like to get out of the city." She grinned. "I prepare the traditional meal for them and charge an arm and a leg for it."

"Money isn't everything," he scolded.

Honey entered the back door and saved her from a lecture. "Ready to go, Uncle Nick? The temperature is dropping fast. It's supposed to freeze tonight."

Amelia saw them off, then went to the office to work on the books. It was getting near the end of the year, and she needed to have the ledgers up to date for the accountant.

Later she planned the festive meal she would serve twelve guests on Thanksgiving Day. For a few minutes, she indulged in a daydream that involved her and Seth and their family sitting down to a huge turkey dinner.

Annoyed, she roamed the house, making sure all was in order. She'd already cleaned the rooms used by Seth and his uncle, in case unexpected visitors showed up. With fresh pine boughs and flowers in each of the six upstairs rooms, the house was ready for the weekend.

Usually such activity brought her pleasure and a sense of contentment, but not tonight. After exercising her ankle, she tried to watch a nature show on television. Finally she changed to her nightgown and robe, turned on the gas fire and strummed soft, mournful ballads on her guitar as the temperature dropped into the twenties and frost changed the landscape to a ghostly white under the waning moon.

At ten she yawned and rose, then froze as a door opened and closed in the front part of the house. The fire danced over the logs, and a chill went up her spine.

"Who is it?" she called from the doorway, phone in hand to dial 911, just in case.

"Seth." He appeared at the corner of the great room. "Sorry, I didn't see a light. I thought you were asleep, so I was trying to be quiet."

"I was just thinking of going to bed. I have to get up early tomorrow."

He came down the hall. She replaced the portable phone on its cradle, turned on the switch of the floor lamp beside the sofa, then returned to the rocker.

His eyes flicked over the room, then her. "Did Uncle Nick get home okay?"

"Yes." She told him of the trip to the doctor's office and that Honey had driven the older man to the ranch. "I assumed you would go to the ranch, too."

"Did you rent my room?" he asked before she'd hardly gotten the words out.

"Well, no. I just didn't expect you."

"Didn't you?"

She looked at the fire, at the frosty darkness outside the windows, at the clock ticking silently on the mantel, and finally at him.

His eyes were fathoms deep, reflecting the firelight like secret pools in glens hidden in a forest.

"The past three days have been long," he said, his voice dropping a register. "And lonely."

She tightened the belt on her robe, her fingers cold and awkward although her heart was suddenly pounding, sending hot blood shooting through her body.

He took a step toward her, then stopped. Questions arched in the air like flaming arrows shooting from him to her, from her to him.

"Complications," she said in warning.

"Yes."

"What if we fall in love?"

He stopped breathing, and she wondered why the possibility of love caused him such anxiety.

He let the trapped breath out with an audible rush. "I'm not promising anything," he said in a low voice, as if the words hurt. "I can't."

She made a decision, knowing that she could never, in some future time of despair, claim she hadn't known the consequences. "All right," she said.

He gazed at her another moment, then stepped forward and swept her into his arms. Carrying her into the bedroom, he whispered, "Sometimes I have dreams about us...and about having a life together."

She stared at him, eyes wide and full of questions.

"Don't ask me anything," he pleaded softly. "Just give me tonight."

When he sat her on the bed, she drew his dear face down to hers. "Tonight," she agreed, and refused to think of all the nights beyond this one when she might be alone again.

Chapter Nine

Seth woke slowly, with a sense of contentment. He wasn't one to linger in bed, but today he didn't want to get up. The reason was in his arms.

Amelia snuggled close to him, one leg nestled between his, an arm thrown over his chest. Her hair brushed the underside of his chin when she moved, and he smoothed it down, liking the silky feel of it.

Her breathing changed.

"Sorry," he murmured. "I didn't mean to awaken you."

"Mmm, I was having a delicious dream." She tugged at his chest hair with her lips.

He tried to recall the last time he'd slept all night with a woman. It wasn't something he usually did.

Amelia felt right in his arms. Too right. He should get up. His office furniture was due to arrive around eleven. He should make sure the place was ready for it.

He didn't move.

"Hungry?" she asked.

"Maybe. For you."

Flipping them over, he reversed their positions and covered her with his body. During the night, her nightgown had been discarded. At some point, he'd helped her into his T-shirt. Now he tugged it out of the way so he could find one delectable nipple and retaliate for her playful tug.

She fought a determined battle, and soon they were breathing hard, the covers in a tangle as they wrestled for supremacy. As an adult, he'd given up play for the serious pursuit of a career. Now he discovered the pure physical exhilaration of using his body in a lover's game.

When they at last rested, he realized he had never felt so alert in mind and body. Each moment was etched into brilliance by the rising sun. He wanted it to last forever.

"Uh, don't you have to work today?" she demanded, her breasts rising and falling against him.

"Yeah. Later." With a slow smile, he held her pinned in position and bent his head until he could flick the pink tip of one breast with his tongue. He did the same to the other until they stood in taut peaks.

"You're beautiful," he said, the words coming

from a place deep inside. He worried about that and what this woman was beginning to mean in his life. He blocked the thought with the will that came from a lifetime of shutting out the past. It was also useful for shutting out the future, he'd found of late.

"So are you," she told him with an ardent catch in her voice as he tasted the treasure again.

He made love to her with a deliberate slow savoring of each moment, each heartbeat. They came together in a natural rhythm, as if created with the same internal tempo that flowed and surged as passion rose to a perfect peak, held, then gently set them down in an afterglow of peace.

"The best," he said. "You're the best."

She kept her eyes closed, but a smile settled at the corners of her mouth. He held her lightly, a treasure so delicate he knew he had to be very careful with her.

The ringing of the telephone finally drove them from the warm bed. They showered and dressed, then ate breakfast before checking the answering machine. They listened as Bertie, the clinic receptionist and bookkeeper, advised him the furniture had arrived.

"Got to go," he said upon hearing the message. "You want to help me arrange things? Can you leave the B and B?"

"Yes, the machine will pick up any messages. I haven't seen where your office will be located."

"Do you remember the old dining room and a room next to it? They'll be my office and conference room. Beau is going to share his receptionist until I'm established. Then we'll see how it goes.''

On the way to the other Victorian, he thought of the night just past and wondered if any woman could love him as he really was and not as the man he'd created, a man who used the Dalton name but had no right to it.

Glancing at Amelia beside him in the truck, one word came to him. *Maybe.*

He mentally shook his head at the false hope. He wasn't a boy, dreaming that life could be wonderful if only he never had to go back to his old life, or see his dad again. If only he could be part of the Dalton family, life would be perfect, he'd thought, filled with the rashness of youth.

So it was. But there was also a price for living in paradise—the fear of being revealed as a fraud.

Amelia and Shelby considered the arrangement of desk and chairs. ''I like it,'' Shelby said.

''Works for me,'' Amelia agreed.

The desk was centered at one end of the room, with a credenza behind it and stately floor-to-ceiling bookcases to each side. The law books and diplomas looked impressive. Two comfortable chairs faced the desk, and a leather sofa and coffee table occupied the other end of the former dining room. In the room next door, a conference table with eight chairs was available.

''Flowers have been arriving since eight this morning,'' Shelby said, gesturing toward the large bouquets and potted plants that filled every corner. "The Chamber of Commerce. The mayor's office. The hardware store. The bank. It's nice living in a place where people appreciate you, isn't it?"

"Yes. It was the same when I opened the B and B."

"Looks as if his first customer has arrived." Shelby nodded toward the side porch that gave access to the private entrance to Seth's new office.

An older man stood there, perhaps in his sixties, dressed in jeans, boots and a denim jacket. His hair was down to his shoulders and covered by a billed cap with an oil company logo on it. With a mustache and a three-day growth of beard, he looked rather seedy and unkempt.

While the man hesitated, Amelia stepped forward and opened the carved Victorian door. "Hi. May I help you?"

"Seth Dalton in?" he asked.

"He isn't here at the moment, but should be back soon." Amelia wondered what to do. "Uh, his receptionist is through that door. If you would like to make an appointment," she added, when the man didn't move.

"I'll catch him later," he said, and headed for the parking lot at the side of the building.

"Would you like to leave your name and number?"

"No," he said without looking back.

Amelia closed the door against a cold west wind. "I'm glad Seth doesn't take criminal cases."

Shelby laughed. "The man was probably a rancher having a dispute with his neighbor over property lines or water rights. I don't think he was comfortable being here. Some old-timers think lawyers are kin to the devil."

"Well, so do I," Amelia said matter-of-factly, then had to smile at the lie. The locals had declared the Dalton orphans the spawn of Satan years ago for their daredevil ways, but when trouble came, the Daltons were the ones who, with no hesitation, stepped forward to help out.

She thought of lying in bed, Seth's arms around her. She'd felt safe there, cherished in a way she'd never known. Her own dark angel, she mused.

His smile had been tinged with emotions she couldn't easily read—longing, bitterness, a certain sad nostalgia—when she'd opened her eyes and found him staring at her.

When Seth returned from errands at the bank and Beau got a break, the men joined Amelia and Shelby for lunch around the conference room table. Raising paper cups, they toasted the new enterprise.

"Oops, I have a meeting this afternoon," Amelia told the others. "Miss Pickford is bringing over a draft of the county history for me to read."

"Are you exercising that ankle?" Beau asked, his keen gaze on her when she rose and hobbled a bit upon taking the first couple of steps.

"She is," Seth declared firmly.

Amelia felt the heat in her face when Beau and Shelby glanced at her in amusement.

''What did I tell you?'' Beau demanded. ''When Seth takes charge, you disobey at your peril.''

Seth stood and took her arm to steady her. ''I'll drive you home.''

''I'd rather walk. I really do need to stretch my legs.'' She paused. ''Will you be at the B and B tonight?''

''Isn't my room available?'' he countered.

''Yes. I thought you might go to the ranch.''

''I spoke to Uncle Nick. He expects me on Saturday morning.''

Feeling self-conscious, Amelia put on a jacket, tucked her purse under her arm and walked out into the wind. Down the block, she passed a black pickup truck. The man who had been looking for Seth sat inside, reading a newspaper. His eyes met hers. She nodded and hurried on.

Miss Pickford arrived at the B and B a few minutes after Amelia. ''It's really cold today. Snow flurries are predicted for tonight,'' the former teacher said, hanging her coat on the hall tree.

Amelia carried a tray from the kitchen. ''I have tea ready. Help yourself. Is anyone else due?''

''Not today. I have the first complete draft of the history put together. I thought each member of the committee should read it, then we'll do revisions and send it to the printer in March.''

Amelia served hibiscus tea and a platter of Marta's raison scones. ''We should have copies for Pioneer Days in June. I hope we sell out.'' She crossed her fingers and laughed ruefully.

"So do I. I would hate to embarrass the historical society by having our big fund-raiser turn out a flop."

They discussed the project in detail, then refilled their cups and relaxed. "I'm glad Seth is opening an office here," Miss Pickford remarked. "The town is growing. We've needed a local attorney for years. And a doctor. Luckily the Daltons are from here, so they have an incentive to come home. Most small towns can't attract professionals of their caliber."

Amelia nodded. It wouldn't be long before the grapevine picked up on an affair between her and Seth. While it was no one's business but theirs, she hated to be the object of gossip. She'd experienced enough speculation about her family as a child. She didn't need more as an adult.

"Were the Daltons good students?" she asked.

"They were. I only taught the two oldest boys before I retired, but I knew the others from Sunday school. Seth was the most serious," Miss Pickford continued, a nostalgic twinkle in her eyes, "and Trevor the most lighthearted. The rest fell somewhere between those two. Veronica was the youngest of the orphans. I worried about her."

Amelia was surprised. "Why?"

"She was around four when she came here. She'd lost her mother and father in less than two years of each other. Then her aunt died and Nick's daughter disappeared. I wondered if her determination to keep up with the Dalton boys was out of fear of being left behind again."

''Abandonment,'' Amelia murmured.

She knew the feeling. Each time her parents had split and she'd been sent to her grandparents, she'd thought she might never see her mom and dad again. She'd adored her grandparents, but she'd felt she was somehow the cause of her parents' troubles.

''I shouldn't admit this, but Seth was my favorite,'' Miss Pickford said after a moment of silence.

''Because he was the best student?''

The older woman shook her head. ''It wasn't only that he was intelligent. He was so earnest, too. He seemed to have an inner code of ethics and sense of fairness that went far beyond most children of his years. Other kids went to him to settle disputes because they knew they could trust his judgment.''

Amelia couldn't deny the sense of pride she took in hearing the former teacher praise Seth.

''He's a good person,'' Miss Pickford finished. ''I hope he finds someone special soon. He's a family man if ever I saw one.''

''He's been wonderful with his uncle,'' Amelia said, ''handling the insurance and medicare forms and all that. He helped me with the legal forms when my grandparents died.''

''It was a lucky day for the historical society when you moved here permanently.'' Miss Pickford pointed to the thick folder on the table. ''I'm not sure we could have gotten this project completed without you.''

''No, no,'' Amelia declared, laughing. ''Teachers

are scary people. We were all afraid not to do exactly as you said.''

She walked the older woman to the door and saw her off. Down the street, she noticed a black pickup. Her heart lurched, then quieted. In a ranching community, black pickups were the transportation of choice.

Seth glanced at his watch for the tenth time in twenty minutes. He looked at the box of records and was tempted to leave them for tomorrow. But tomorrow was a busy day and this was the last set of records to be put away.

''You got a heavy date?'' Beau asked.

Seth looked at his brother.

''You've been clock watching for the past hour.''

''Oh.'' Seth tried to think of an excuse. His mind went totally blank.

Beau chuckled.

''What?'' Seth asked. He'd always found it annoying when others acted as if they had a big secret they weren't sharing.

''You.'' Beau finished storing the records in the special lockable file vaults and flattened the box brought up from Boise. ''You've got it bad.''

Anger flashed through Seth, taking him by surprise. He quelled it with an iron will, not liking that the emotion had gotten away from him. Control was the secret of a successful life.

''Not me,'' he said, keeping his tone easy, amused.

"Where are you staying tonight?"

"At the B and B."

"Exactly." Beau chuckled.

Heat burned through Seth again. Again, he had to exert his will to control unexpected emotion. He stuffed the last folders into the hanging files and closed the cabinet.

"You're implying there's something between me and Amelia?"

Beau shrugged. "Shelby and Honey say so. I've always trusted women's intuition."

Seth heaved a sigh, muttered an expletive and found neither did the least bit of good. "There's nothing…I mean, there *is,* but it isn't what you think."

"I think you're head over heels and scared to death to admit it." Beau tossed a wry smile his way as he stacked the empty moving cartons on top of others they had emptied. "It isn't so bad, not if the other person feels the same. Shelby says Amelia does."

It took a second for Seth to recognize the painful leap in his chest as hope. He squashed it mercilessly. "Just what I need," he said with calculated cynicism, "another entanglement right when I'm trying to establish a new business. I'm not convinced the town can support a full-time attorney, much less his family."

Beau obviously didn't see a problem. "It wouldn't have to. Amelia has her own business."

Pictures flashed on Seth's mental screen. His father snatching his mom's purse and taking the tips she'd earned working long hours as a waitress. His mom sneaking food home to Seth because there were no groceries in the house. The beatings he and his mom had endured when there was no money to feed his father's vices.

''I would never live off a woman.'' This time he couldn't keep the bitter anger from his tone of voice.

Beau hesitated, then said softly, ''Don't let a good thing get away. It's much nicer to hold a sweet loving woman close to your heart than false pride.''

Scenes from that morning overlaid scenes from the distant past and became snarled like tangled yarns running through his mind. He spoke without thinking. ''Pride is a luxury I've never been able to afford. When you've lived on the edge, your stomach flat against your backbone, believe me, pride isn't a factor.''

Beau took a step forward and got right in his face. ''So what the hell is?'' he asked. ''What's eating you? The move is going fine, you'll soon have more business than you can handle and you know it, there's a beautiful woman interested in you, and yet you act like Saint Joan being led to the stake. When you're not acting like Attila the Hun on a rampage, that is.''

''Thanks for the evaluation,'' Seth said, just as angrily. ''I'll put you down as a reference next time I need one.''

Beau paced to the window and turned. ''Sorry. It's just that lately you've become withdrawn, moody. It isn't like you." He grinned. "Falling in love isn't the end of the world as you know it. In fact, it might be better."

Seth knew what heaven felt like in his arms. He also knew he had no right to it. How could he ask a woman to take his name when it wasn't rightfully his to give?

A soft knock sounded on the door to the reception room, then the door opened. Shelby and Nicky stood there.

"Uh, dinner is ready," she said. "Would you care to join us?" she asked Seth.

He shook his head and managed a smile. "I'm not very good company at present." He stooped to the boy's eye level. "Hey, how's my favorite nephew?"

"Fine."

The five-year-old reminded Seth of himself at that age, painfully shy and distrustful of the world. The boy's mother had disappeared and his grandmother had died, leaving him an orphan. He'd been left with Beau, who hadn't known he'd had a son. The Daltons thought something similar had happened to Seth—that Job Dalton was his real father and hadn't known about his son.

Little did they know…

"Gimme a high five," he said to the youngster.

They slapped palms and exchanged solemn smiles. Seth rose and headed for the door, an ache in his chest for all the children in the world who were hurt by the adults they were supposed to trust.

He touched Beau's shoulder as he opened the door. "Don't worry. It's just a phase."

"I'm a good listener," Beau replied. "We had to take a class for it in medical school."

"Yeah, just as we did in law school."

They parted laughing, but the amusement faded as Seth drove the short distance to the B and B. His heart kicked in a furious pace as he parked at the side of the neat old Victorian.

Standing under an oak that was probably older than the house, he took in the scene, deciding it would make a great postcard. Night had fallen and the lights on the front porch gleamed in welcome to the weary traveler. Better yet was the glow from the tall windows, indicating warmth inside and that someone was waiting....

He took a step forward, eagerness humming through his blood. Amelia... "Seth Dalton?" A voice spoke from the shadows.

Seth whirled, hands fisted as he tried to peer into the darkness. "Yeah. Who are you?"

A man stepped from behind the yew shrubs onto the gravel driveway and came forward. He stopped three feet from Seth. Seth opened the pickup door, causing the inside light to come on.

The man raised a hand to shield his face, but Seth had already recognized the sharp features. "You," he said.

"So you know who I am," his father concluded.

Seth shoved the door closed and said nothing.

"Not a very warm welcome for your old man."

Seth noted the whining undertone and tensed. He'd heard it before when his dad was trying to wheedle something out of another person. Some things were never forgotten.

"What do you want?" he asked.

"Where can we talk?"

Seth didn't want the old con man near Amelia. He gestured toward the carriage house. His father nodded and followed him along the drive. Inside the office for the dance school, Seth turned on the light, then sat on the edge of the desk, his pose deceptively relaxed as he waited.

Frank Maguire was sixty-five and his face showed it. Once as muscular as his son, he now had a dissipated appearance, that of an athlete who'd gone to seed. Although skinny, he had a paunch hanging over his belt. His eyes were bloodshot and shifty, the lines around them indicating anger and scorn rather than laughter.

After a lengthy silence, he finally spoke. "Not pleased to see a poor relative invade your posh life here?"

"How did you find me?" Seth asked, curious but not particularly interested. This man was from a part of his life that was forever closed, as far as he was concerned.

"I always remember names. You put down Seth Dalton on the sign-in sheet that time you came to the prison."

Seth snorted. "You didn't know who I was."

"Not then," Frank admitted, then looked sorrowful. "I'm sorry for that, son. I'd been in prison a long time. You and your mom never visited."

One thing Seth had observed well over the years were the ways people dissembled. He almost laughed at the attempt to put a guilt trip on him for not visiting. His only regret was going to the prison that one time after he got out of law school. He didn't know why he had, other than maybe a last lingering hope that the years had changed his father into a decent, caring man.

It had been a stupid trip, the last foolish vestige of that boy who'd wanted a father who was honorable.

But the con who'd greeted him had been the same man he'd known in his youth, one with a grudge against the world, as if the rest of humanity owed him something.

Seth could tell him that life didn't agree. A man worked for his place in the scheme of things. He acted with integrity and built a reputation as a trustworthy person. Frank Maguire had never learned that lesson.

"So you've found me, now what?" Seth asked, sure he knew what was coming.

"I'm broke," the old man said with fake humility. "A man my age, it's hard to start over."

"You've been out of prison what? Nine years? What have you been doing all that time?"

"Trying to make a living. No one wants to give an ex-con a break." The whine had returned.

"What do you know how to do?" Seth asked.

"Maybe there's something you can find in another town."

Frank's head came up. His eyes, as dark as Seth's own, glinted with anger. "I need money."

"But not a job. I see."

The old man gestured vaguely, a threat in his manner. "You got it nice, being a lawyer and all and part of the Dalton family. I heard the story of how you got here, too, about finding your long lost dad, then losing him in the avalanche. It's a real sad story."

The hidden core of darkness opened inside Seth. Something cold and contemptible spread from it, filling him with a festering rage. He looked at his hands and for the first time understood how a person could want to strangle an enemy. He wanted to rip the beating heart out of this evil person from his past. He wanted to smash the sly, grinning face with a rock until it never smiled again.

Doing so would make him as bad as his father. Like father, like son? It was a legacy he'd tried to live down all his life, but at this moment, he wanted to obliterate the old man from the face of the earth.

"Get out of my sight," he said now with deadly calm.

"Don't get hoity-toity with me—"

"Now!" Seth warned. "Or so help me God, I'll make you wish you'd never heard the name Seth Dalton. Get out of Lost Valley and don't come back."

Frank pulled his cap lower over his eyes. "It's a

free country,'' he mumbled as a parting shot, then hastened out the door when Seth took a step toward him.

Long after the specter from the past had gone and his rickety vehicle had disappeared down the street, Seth sat with one hip propped on the desk, not conscious of anything but the violent rage ebbing and flowing in him. Slowly he brought his thoughts under control and rose, slowly, stiffly, like an old man bent under years of harsh living, and went to the Victorian.

He paused at the door of his room and listened to soft music coming from the back part of the house. He had only to go down this hall, turn left, walk a few more paces and he would find paradise.

Shaking his head slightly, he went inside the empty room and closed the door. He opened his hands and studied them as if they were foreign to his body. These were the hands that had touched *her,* that had caressed the dark warmth of her hair and experienced the smoothness of her skin and found the moist honey of her welcoming body.

Tonight these hands had wanted to kill a man.

He shed his clothing and got into the single bed. He could feel the old agony inside, the grief that had shredded his soul as a boy and now as a man. Out of the rage and sorrow, out of the terrible need to destroy and to weep, one thought stood out clearly from the rest.

Paradise wasn't for the likes of him.

Chapter Ten

Friday morning, Amelia woke shortly before five-thirty. Her sleep had been restless, and now she remembered why. Seth hadn't come to her last night when he got in from his new office. The bed had felt lonely.

Lying there, she heard the heat come on and start to warm the old house to its daytime temperature. She stayed in bed until the furnace clicked off. Still tired, she rose and dressed and headed for the kitchen. Guests were expected that evening and she had things to do.

Seth was in the kitchen when she entered.

"Oh. Good morning," she said. "I wondered if you got in okay last night. I didn't hear you...."

She let the words trail into silence. He didn't owe her an explanation for his absence.

He glanced at her over his coffee mug, then took a drink before replying. "Yeah, I got in okay."

Nodding, she prepared oatmeal and toast.

"Don't fix any for me," he said. "I'm not staying."

"It's rather early to go to the office, isn't it?"

"I'm heading for the ranch. I've decided to stay there and…and keep an eye on things."

She noted the hesitation. "Is your uncle worse? He's welcome to stay here if you think—"

"He's fine. I just need to sort through some things."

At the repressive tone, Amelia shut up. It didn't take a genius to know Seth didn't want to talk about his reasons, not with her at any rate.

Funny how a person could slip so quickly into the patterns of the past. She'd learned as a child to hide all emotion as her parents went through their ups and downs, so frequently that life with them had resembled a roller coaster at times. She'd never expected it with Seth.

"I see," she said with no display of emotion, taking her place on a stool and picking up the spoon. She ate quietly without tasting the meal.

"I doubt it."

The biting cynicism got to her. "Then why don't you explain it in simple terms that even I can get?"

She pressed her lips together, but the hateful words were already spoken. Regret followed on the heels of her outburst. Anger did absolutely no good, either.

"I'm sorry," she said before he could speak. "It's none of my business."

He touched her hand and withdrew. "I'm the one who should apologize. Things have gotten complicated. I need some space to think."

The gentleness of his manner didn't override the bitter undercurrent in the words. "I don't think I understand."

He sighed. "I know. I can't explain, not now." He rose. "I'm leaving. Don't hold the room for me."

She nodded and even managed a farewell smile. A minute later the side door closed as he left. She heard his truck crank up, then the sound of the motor in the early morning air faded as he drove away. The finality of his leaving sank into her heart amid a heavy weight of sorrow and unanswered questions.

"Never again," she said at last into the silence. "Never again."

Seth was aware of his uncle's scrutiny Saturday morning. He rose right after the meal. "I have to go to the office, then I thought I'd work on the lodge."

"I'll help out," Trevor volunteered. "I want to finish priming the walls of the downstairs rooms."

Uncle Nick snorted. "Good. I'm tired of the gloomy faces around here. Both of you look as if Death paid a call and is coming back for you before the month is over."

Seth and Trevor glanced at each other. Neither smiled or made a quip in reply.

"Sometimes it helps to talk," the older man said.

Neither nephew said anything.

"Humph." Their uncle snorted again in obvious irritation.

"Nothing wrong here," Trevor said, gathering his dishes and taking them to the kitchen.

"I'm fine, too," Seth said.

"Why don't you bring Amelia out to dinner tonight? I want to thank her for letting me stay at her place."

"She has guests this weekend. Besides, it was a business arrangement. I paid her for our rooms."

His uncle looked thunderous. "Now you've insulted her. She did that as a friend."

"She runs a business," Seth said. He tried to erase the harshness from his voice. "I didn't think it right to use her place without paying."

He followed the older man into the kitchen and put his dishes into the dishwasher when Trevor finished.

"I'm off," Trevor said, and headed out.

"Me, too." Seth started for the door.

"Don't let pride or a misunderstanding get in the way of happiness," Uncle Nick advised.

Seth stopped and turned. Looking into the shrewd blue eyes, he wondered if he should tell the truth—that his real father was in town and demanding money. "Sometimes things are beyond your control," he said.

His uncle nodded. ''Sometimes a resolution is easier than you think. A simple conversation can often clear the air.''

Seth realized the older man thought he and Amelia had had a lover's quarrel. The blackness inside him shifted as rage arose. His father had traced him to Amelia's place. Seth wanted distance between her and the ex-con. That's why he'd left, why he'd had to hurt her. To keep her safe.

''What's wrong, son?''

The concern in Uncle Nick's face was almost Seth's undoing. He wanted to confess everything, every lie and every misconception he'd perpetuated upon this trusting, caring man. He wanted to ask the wise old man how to rid himself of the burden of Frank Maguire and how to hold the love of the one woman he wanted more than life itself.

The words crowded into his throat, but he didn't utter them. ''Nothing,'' he said, and felt the lie as a hot stab in his soul. ''I'll see you tonight.''

In town, he returned some calls to clients and one to his partner in Boise. After hanging up, he sat at the desk and gazed around the office. Beau, Shelby, Amelia, Bertie...all of them had participated in the arrangement of furniture and diplomas. He could recall their laughter as they'd chatted and made suggestions, and he realized their friendship was more valuable than diamonds to him.

What would they think if they learned the truth?

He rubbed his face wearily. It never paid to give in to blackmail, or else you became a conspirator with the blackmailer and were trapped in your own deceit for a lifetime. On the other hand, if he admitted the facts, then everyone would know Nick Dalton had lied.

Unless Seth could convince everyone that he was the one who'd lied and convinced the older man it was the truth?

Or he could pay off his father, move to Denver or L.A. and start over, putting distance between himself and the Daltons. Over time, he would see them less and less frequently, until finally they forgot about the intruder into the family.

But he would never forget them and the good life he'd found in this small corner of the world.

After closing the office, he drove to the resort, where he joined Trevor and Zack, both already hard at work. He wouldn't be around for the grand opening, he realized.

"What do you want me to do?" he asked.

"How about helping us paint?" Zack suggested.

The three worked together with the ease that came from years of cooperation under their uncle's direction. Seth would miss these cousins he'd claimed twenty-two years ago.

"Have you noticed how quiet Trevor is?" Zack asked when he and Seth were finishing the dining room and Trevor had moved on to the reception area.

"Yeah. Travis mentioned it."

"It's more than getting his ribs busted in the rodeo,'' Zack continued. ''You think he met someone?''

''And fell in love and lost her?'' Seth asked dryly.

Zack gave him a surprised glance. ''I never knew you were a cynic about things of the heart,'' he said slowly.

Seth shrugged.

''Something wrong between you and Amelia?''

''No. There's nothing at all between us.''

''Honey says there is.''

''She's an authority on the subject?'' he asked in a snarl.

''Hey,'' Zack said. ''This is your ol' cuz you're talking to. What's wrong, man?''

''Not a damn thing.'' Seth tossed the paintbrush into a bucket of water.

''Well, pardon me,'' Zack snapped.

Seth walked out before he did something he'd regret—like confess all and ask for help.

No. This was his problem. He would handle it.

Amelia saw her guests off on Sunday shortly before noon. By two, she had the beds changed, the linens washed and dried and the old house dusted and tidy.

She went to her sitting room with a sandwich and a cup of tea. She ate, then exercised her ankle. After finishing the book she'd been reading, she sat and gazed out the window, her thoughts vague.

Clouds gathered over the western peaks, and she wondered if another storm was on the way. The snow had melted from the streets in town, but still nestled in drifts under the trees and other shady spots, gathering soot from the wood fires that warmed the homes in the county.

The Seven Devils were white and stately, though. She tried to recall the individual names. He-Devil. She-Devil. The Devil's Tooth. Those were the easy ones. Mount Ogre. Mount Baal. What else? The Goblin.

Finally she retrieved a brochure she kept for her guests and checked the final name. The Tower of Babel was the peak she could never remember.

Her grandmother had often teased her grandfather about it, saying that the Tower of Babel in the Bible referred to men and women, who never spoke the same language although they used the same words.

Amelia had thought that was so funny at the time. Now she admitted it was closer to the truth than she'd realized as a child. The bond she'd felt between her and Seth had obviously been imaginary on her part. She'd thought they were falling in love, that he'd felt it, too.

She frowned as she considered the events of the past month. The attraction was real, and it went beyond the physical, but something stood between them. Only he knew what it was.

Helplessness gripped her. She'd faced a similar situation with her parents. She'd been blown here and there by the turbulence of their marriage, but she'd had no say in the outcome of their lives. It was the same with Seth.

When she'd come here to live, she'd vowed not to allow herself to be at the mercy of other's whims. That resolve was still with her. Whatever Seth's problem, he had to come to terms with it before there was hope for them.

She napped, then went for a walk. The clouds hung over the mountains but hadn't moved into the valley. Her breath formed a cloud each time she exhaled, though, and she zipped the thick parka right up to her chin to keep the cold out.

The trail around the lake traced a curving path between the water and the buildings on the west side. From the resort being built by the Daltons, she heard the whacks of a hammer. Her heart thudded in time to the blows. Seth usually worked there with his cousins each weekend.

Stopping, she surveyed the impressive structure. Next to it was a tiny white cottage owned by Beau and Shelby. To Amelia, Seth seemed like the resort—big and strong and overpowering, while she saw herself as the cottage—small and insignificant in the scheme of things.

She smiled at the whimsy and wondered if it indicated an inferiority complex on her part. Or maybe it was telling it like it was. As she turned to retrace her steps, a man came out of the huge lodge.

Seth stopped on the patio, his eyes on her.

She didn't move as he walked across the sloping lawn and stopped three feet away.

"I thought that was you," he said, his eyes restless as they moved over her face. ‘‘It’s cold to be out for a walk.’’

‘‘I’m exercising my ankle,’’ she said, hating it that she sounded defensive, as if she needed an excuse to be there.

‘‘Good.’’

She was puzzled as he glanced all around the area, then back at her, worry in his dark gaze. ‘‘I’m just going back,’’ she said, and set off along the path toward town.

He fell in beside her. ‘‘I’ll walk with you.’’

‘‘I don’t need an escort.’’

He didn’t reply, but neither did he let her go alone. He didn’t speak as they crossed the park at the community center and continued down Main Street to the lane where the B and B was located. They climbed the few steps to the front porch.

She’d replaced the old swing where they’d kissed so passionately so long ago, but the new one was identical. Amelia had hitched it up under the rafters to protect it from the winter weather. Come summer, she would let it down again so her guests could use it. Forcing her gaze from it, she opened the door.

‘‘You should keep that locked,’’ he said.

‘‘Why?’’

He didn’t answer for a minute, then said, ‘‘Because.’’

‘‘That’s a good reason.’’

‘‘You don’t know who might come along.’’

‘‘Right. We have so many suspicious characters in town.’’

He gestured in exasperation. "This place is so wide-open, anyone could walk in. You need to be more careful."

"I run a business here, remember? The door is unlocked because people are supposed to come in."

His frown assured her he didn't care for her reply. She shrugged, her own temper fraying at his attitude.

"I've got to get back," he finally said. "Take care."

It sounded more like an order than a wish for her good health. She nodded and watched him depart the way they'd come, then she walked into the house and was immediately aware of a presence.

A man stood in front of the reception area.

The hair on her neck stood up when she recognized him. It was the man who'd come to Seth's office the other day, the seedy rancher or whoever he was. She didn't recall seeing him in the area before he'd turned up at the law office. He held the advertising brochure she'd had made for the B and B.

"May I help you?" she asked, hanging up the parka.

"You got a room available?"

She was tempted to say no, but that was stupid. After all, this was a business. "Yes. How long are you interested in staying?"

"Dunno," he said, slurring the words.

"All the rooms are reserved beginning Wednesday night and going through the weekend."

He held up the advertisement. "This says the

rooms start at fifty dollars. That the cheapest you got?"

"Yes, and I'm afraid that one is already spoken for," she said, not exactly lying. The single room was Seth's, in case he needed to stay in town.

"Huh," the man said.

She didn't like his eyes and the way they took in everything, from her to the clocks and the antique silver service on the buffet. "There's a place on the lake that has cabins and trailers. You go past the Crow's Nest Restaurant and turn left. You'll see a sign for the Angler's Haven."

He nodded. "You need any help around here? I'm good at repairs and handyman stuff."

So he was down on his luck. That's what she'd suspected. She suppressed the ready sympathy. "I'm sorry. I already have someone who helps in the summer. Winter is the slow season around here."

"I've noticed."

"Other than fishing and hiking in the summer, this is mostly ranching country," she added, in case he was thinking of settling here.

He slapped the billed cap against his leg as if to knock dust off. It was the one with the oil company logo. That reminded her of a Help Wanted sign she'd seen recently.

"There's a gas station on the highway north of here. They often need help," she said.

"Maybe I'll check it out."

He headed toward the door while Amelia breathed a sigh of relief. There was something about him, something more than the down-at-the-heels seediness of his appearance, that gave her an uneasy sensation in the pit of her stomach.

It came to her after he left. His pickup hadn't been in the parking area in front of the house. Where had he left it? And why?

After he disappeared down the street on foot, she locked the three outside doors and checked the windows in each room, upstairs and down, to make sure they were secure.

Feeling foolish, she heated a bowl of soup and ate in front of the fire in her private quarters. At ten, when she went to bed, she noticed the storm had crept quietly down the mountainside. Snow was falling in a thick flurry over the land. She hoped the old man had found a place to stay, and tried not to feel guilty that he couldn't afford a room at the B and B and that she hadn't wanted him.

Monday, Tuesday and Wednesday were filled to the brim with activity. Amelia divided her time between shopping, preparing for guests and cooking the most delicious recipes she could find in magazines and cookbooks.

She hung wreaths of evergreen boughs wrapped with ribbon and strung with fruit, nuts and cinnamon sticks, then baked cookies and stored them in the decorative tins once used by her grandmother. She bought a dozen poinsettias and placed them at the front door and in the great room.

Those were her days. The nights were a different story. The loneliness was almost unbearable.

By ten on Wednesday evening, the house was ready and her visitors had arrived—two families of four each and two couples, the twelve of them related by blood or marriage. Amelia served tea and cocoa and cookies to welcome them.

Leaving the great room filled with quiet talk and laughter, she retired to her quarters.

Nick Dalton smiled at the trill of feminine laughter coming from the kitchen. Roni and the three wives, as he thought of the young women married to his nephews, were in the midst of Thanksgiving dinner preparations.

The men were in the paddock, checking out a new stallion Trevor had bought to improve the lines of the cutting horses the ranch raised and sold. All except Beau, who'd had to go to the office for a medical emergency, and Seth, who was in the ranch office going over the accounts and bills.

Shaking his head at the human capacity for foolishness, Nick entered the kitchen. ''When is this meal going to get on the table?'' he asked with mock ferocity.

Roni blew a kiss at him. ''An hour, max.''

''Any sign of Janis, Keith and the baby?'' Alison asked as she removed a pumpkin pie from the oven.

''Not yet,'' he answered.

Alison was married to Travis, and her sister, brother-in-law and baby nephew, who lived on an adjoining ranch, were invited to the big meal. Nick liked having friends as well as family join them for the holiday. Milly had, too.

For a moment, he was lost in memories of his wife. She'd died more than twenty-two years ago, but sometimes it seemed only last week that he'd lost her.

A few times of late, he'd thought he'd heard her laughter in the distance when the wind was just right. Once or twice, as he was waking, he heard voices belonging to his beloved Milly and their child, the merry, talkative Tink, coming down the hall.

But it was only an old man's dream.

The telephone rang, bringing him back to the present. He heard Seth answer.

"Janis and her bunch are on the way." His nephew called out the news after he hung up.

"Thanks," Alison called back.

Roni frowned. "Seth needs to take a day off."

"I agree," Honey said.

Shelby, the newest bride of the three, nodded, too. "Maybe he's trying not to think of Amelia."

Nick, too, thought Seth was fighting an attraction for the lovely B and B owner. He couldn't figure out what was the matter with the boy. Amelia was attracted to him, too. A person with one eye could see the tension between them.

Roni snapped her fingers. "She should come out to the ranch and have dinner." She turned and looked at him. "What do you think, Uncle Nick?"

"Well, that would be nice. Do you want me to call her?"

His niece considered, shook her head and smiled. "I think we should go to town and kidnap her," she declared.

She looked so much like the young Tink when she was thinking up mischief that it caused his heart to ache.

"Do you think she would come?" Shelby asked doubtfully.

"She might if we suddenly showed up," Roni told her.

Honey spoke. "Amelia won't leave her guests without someone to take care of them."

The four women looked at him as if seeking a solution. He had an idea. "Let's see if Marta knows someone who will help out."

"Great! Would you call?"

Nodding to his niece, Nick went to the wall phone in the kitchen. Roni looked up the number. Soon it was arranged that Marta's cousin's oldest girl would go the B and B and do the dishes or whatever so Amelia would be free. Nick promised an exorbitant fee for her services and hung up, feeling the money was well spent.

"Who's going with me?" Roni asked.

The three wives looked at each other. "We are," they said almost in unison.

Nick shook his head. "It's almost an hour to town and another one back. Call Beau and have him stop by for her on his way home."

"Right. He can tell her Uncle Nick wants her to come out so he can repay her for taking care of him," Shelby suggested. "I'll call him."

They got Beau on the phone before he left the clinic. He promised to pick up Amelia if the women promised to protect him from Seth's possible fury. They all shouted that they would when Shelby relayed this request.

Nick grinned when Seth appeared from down the hall, coffee mug in hand. "What's going on?" he asked with a tolerant smile, but a trace of annoyance in his eyes.

"Nothing," Roni said.

The wives solemnly agreed.

Their manner was suspicious. When Seth looked at him, Uncle Nick shrugged as if he hadn't a clue.

"You got a minute to go over the records?" Seth finally asked, dismissing the women and their merriment.

His uncle nodded and followed him to the office.

"All the ledgers are up to date in the computer. I've printed out a balance sheet. The horse sale brought us well into the black—"

"Give that money to Zack and the twins. They did everything," Uncle Nick said.

"You can do that if you like, but as owner of the land, you're entitled to one-third of the profits."

"The boys have bought almost half the ranch," Nick reminded him. "You and Beau and Roni agreed to that."

"Right. We have careers that don't allow a lot of

extra time for taking care of the land and livestock. You helped us through school. It was a fair exchange.''

''Do you think so?''

Seth looked up from the piece of paper. ''I know so,'' he said quietly. ''You're the most evenhanded person I've ever known.''

''Don't paint a picture of me as a saint. I've never been that,'' the older man advised lightly, his gaze penetrating as he observed Seth.

Seth wanted to protest, but he didn't. The rancher had never had any illusions about his state of grace.

But of all the people Seth knew, this one man didn't need saintliness, he reflected. Uncle Nick had compassion and integrity and all the qualities that Seth had tried to find within himself since coming to the Seven Devils Ranch. He'd rather cut off his right arm than see disappointment in those pure blue eyes that looked right into a person's soul and saw only good.

Which was why, he supposed, he couldn't yet bring himself to tell his uncle about Frank Maguire. Seth didn't doubt Uncle Nick would take it upon himself to throttle the man for threatening the orphan under Nick's protection, even if that waif was now a grown man.

With the older man's medical history, Seth didn't want him upset in any way, especially not by an ex-con out for all he could get. Seth felt the weight settle more firmly on his shoulders. This was his problem. He would have to figure it out.

A burst of laughter from the kitchen brightened the atmosphere. ''The gals are in good humor today,'' he said, forcing a lightness he was far from feeling.

To his surprise, Uncle Nick frowned and looked worried. ''I hope they aren't stirring the pot too much,'' he said in cryptic tones.

Seth was still trying to figure that out when his uncle returned to the kitchen.

Chapter Eleven

Amelia took two pain pills and plopped on the kitchen stool with an expelled breath. Her ankle throbbed like fire. Yep, it was swollen, she saw when she eased her sock down.

At least all the work was done. She'd had the big meal ready at one o'clock sharp. As usual, she'd served buffet-style, except for the bowls that couldn't be squeezed in around the twenty-five pound turkey, honey-cured ham, two kinds of dressing, cranberry sauce, cranberry-orange relish, gravy and mashed potatoes. The extra vegetables she'd loaded on a tray and taken around the tables.

One of the children had left a toy truck on the floor. Naturally, she hadn't noticed it. She'd stepped on the toy and stumbled. She'd managed to keep from falling or dropping the tray, but she'd twisted her ankle again. Damn.

"Hello," a masculine voice said from the doorway.

Her heart gave a gigantic leap, then settled down when she saw it was Beau Dalton. "Hello yourself." She gave him a smile and slipped her sock over the aching foot. "What are you doing in town?"

"A kid fell on his noggin and split it open. I put twelve stitches in, gave him a lollipop and his parents tranquilizers and sent them home. Here, let me see that," he said, squatting in front of her and reaching for her foot.

There was nothing she could do to hide the fact that she'd overdone. The puffy flesh gave her away.

Beau whistled and shook his head. "I can tell you've been resting as ordered," he said wryly.

"I haven't had any problem before today," she told him, not wanting to admit she'd wrenched her ankle in case he reported it to Seth. "It was the dinner and all. The guests had been scheduled for months, almost a year. I couldn't cancel."

He nodded in understanding. "I thought that might be the case. I brought a remedy. Two, actually. Caitlynn, can you come here for a minute?"

Amelia recognized Marta's cousin's oldest girl when she came to the kitchen door. "Hi, Caitlynn," she said, and looked questioningly at Beau.

''She's taking over for you. She'll wait on your guests and wash the dishes and straighten up.''

''No, no, that's all right. I can handle it. I've put the desserts on a table, so the guests can help themselves.'' She smiled at the teenager. ''You should be with your family today. I know your mom and Marta have prepared a feast.''

''We already ate,'' Caitlynn said. ''I like your place here. I think I'd like to have my own business, too, so I can be my own boss.''

''See?'' Beau demanded of Amelia. ''She needs the experience for her career planning. Now for the second remedy.''

He pulled a bandage from his pocket, removed her loafer and sock and proceeded to wrap her ankle. After that, he made an ice pack from a plastic bag, put her sock and shoe on, then used another stretchy bandage to hold the ice pack in place around her ankle. ''That should do it,'' he decided in a satisfied tone, checking his work.

''Thanks. I think,'' she said.

Definitely amused, he announced, ''Now it's time to go.''

She gave him a blank look.

''Uncle Nick expects you for dinner.''

Her heart did its leaping act again. ''Tell him thanks, but I can't. Really.''

''Really, you can,'' Beau said, mocking her gently. He became serious. ''Uncle Nick insists. He wants to thank you for letting him stay here.''

The heat rose in her face. "There's no need. Seth paid for their rooms, so everything is taken care of."

Beau frowned, then chuckled. "That brother of mine has a hard head. You've probably noticed."

She wasn't sure what to say, so she nodded.

Caitlynn picked up the coffeepot when the machine gave its last gurgle. "I'll see if anyone wants more," she said. "Don't worry about anything. With a family as big as mine, everyone has to pitch in at mealtime. I know what to do."

"See?" Beau said when the teenager left them. "Come on. Uncle Nick won't let the rest of us eat until you're at the table. He's declared you the guest of honor."

Amelia didn't see any graceful way to decline without being rude. "I'll need my coat and purse."

"Tell me where they are," he ordered. "I'll get them."

A few minutes later, she told her guests goodbye and left Caitlynn in charge. Not without trepidation, she limped to Beau's vehicle and, with his hand on her arm, got inside.

Then she fretted all the way to Seven Devils Ranch.

"Don't look so worried," Beau advised, helping her out of the SUV and up the steps of the old-fashioned porch. "Uncle Nick won't let Seth unleash his fangs."

"Seth and I are friends," she said airily, going inside while Beau held the door for her.

Her confidence wavered when all conversation

stopped and everyone turned to check out the new arrivals.

"Amelia, glad you could make it," Uncle Nick said, coming forward to take her hand and urge her on into the living room. He gallantly hung up her parka and had her store the purse on a shelf of the bookcase. "I think you know everyone here," he continued. "Have you met Alison's sister and her family?"

"Yes, at the wedding." She returned the couple's greetings. "Goodness, is that the baby? He's grown a foot since summer."

Roni came forward and gave her a hug. "I'm so glad you could come. Now everyone is here, and we can eat."

"We'll have a blessing," Uncle Nick said. "Seth," he called, "it's time. Leave that stuff for another day."

His tone didn't brook an argument. Amelia wasn't surprised when Seth appeared at once from down the hall. Her heart lurched crazily when he spotted her.

A frown crossed his face and was gone like vapor in the rising sun, leaving no expression at all. She realized he hadn't known she was joining them… and that he didn't like it one iota that she had.

To her horror, tears rushed to her eyes and blood rushed to her face, making her hot and miserable and embarrassed at being there.

"Let us pray," Uncle Nick said.

She bowed her head, grateful for the respite. The older man said a lengthy prayer. By the end, she was in control of her emotions once more.

"Come," Uncle Nick told her. "We'll go to the table and let these young'uns wait on us."

Although she smiled, she admitted she did feel like an old woman as she hobbled to the festively set table. She figured she would have to stay at least two hours before she could plead fatigue and ask to be taken home.

Seth ended up directly across the table from Amelia. He was pretty sure that was by design, thanks to Roni. Each time he glanced up he couldn't help but see Amelia's face, the red-brown hair neatly tamed by a green scrunchy at the back of her neck, and the delectable lips enhanced with a deep coral color.

She wore hunter-green slacks and a sweater of the same color, with white Nordic designs of reindeer prancing across her breasts in a band that drew his gaze there again and again. It was with an effort that he kept his eyes mostly on his plate.

He had also noted the slight limp that she tried to conceal. That, plus the fact that she had a bulge indicating an ice pack around her ankle, worried him. She was obviously in pain, although she smiled and chatted with her usual cheerfulness.

Roni nudged him. "Why so quiet, oh great stone face?"

He managed a casual shrug. ''Who can get a word in amidst all the magpie chatter around here?''

The men agreed with this assessment, bringing protests from the women.

''You all talk at once,'' Zack pointed out. ''I never have understood how women could do that and still seem to know what everybody else is saying.''

''Female brains have parallel processors,'' Roni informed him, gesturing loftily to indicate it was no problem.

''Is she implying that men have one-track minds?'' Beau asked the other men indignantly.

She grinned. ''You said it, brother, not I.''

Seth smiled as the group laughed. His eyes met Amelia's light blue ones across the table. A shaft of longing went through him, so strong it nearly made him groan aloud. He gritted his teeth and waited it out.

The meal went on forever. He took some of whatever was passed by him and ate without noticing the flavor. Uncle Nick and Amelia discussed recipes, while at the other end of the table there was an argument about the new stallion's bloodlines and how good they were.

''You're not having much fun,'' Roni murmured, leaning close as she buttered a hot roll.

''Sure I am.'' He smiled and hoped it wasn't a grimace. ''I always enjoy the family get-togethers.''

''Right. That's why, when no one is watching, you look as if you've just had a root canal.'' She hesitated, then said, "Why don't you tell her how you feel?"

A boulder settled on his chest. "I don't know what you're talking about."

"Amelia. And you know it," she retorted sotto voce. She sighed. "Sorry. I just hate to see you let happiness slip right through your fingers. Don't you think you could be happy with her?" she asked.

Happy with her? Was there any sorrow in paradise?

No, he answered silently, but it was a place he couldn't go. He studied Amelia, aware that she avoided his gaze as she talked to his uncle.

"Yes, I could be happy," he finally said.

"Well?" his half sister prodded.

He shook his head, unable to explain. Looking into Roni's Dalton-blue eyes with the worry showing in their depths, he felt guilt eat at him. She had accepted him as a brother from the first. After the tragedy of the avalanche, she'd clung to him and Beau in equal measure.

Who could help responding to that trust? He'd loved her as his little sister from that moment. At times, it seemed as if he'd had no life before Roni and Beau, Uncle Nick and the cousins had become part of his.

The specter of his father appeared in his inner vision. The old con man was still around. Seth had spotted him in town, on foot, which seemed odd. Seth had seen the black pickup parked out at one of the trailers at the Angler's Haven. Uneasiness hit him now like a cold ball of snow on the back of his neck.

He had to stay away from Amelia. Simply put, he didn't know what Frank might get it into his head to do if the old man thought Seth was involved with her.

Anger swept through him at the thought of her being hurt because of knowing him.

At that moment, Amelia looked his way. He couldn't summon even a pretense of a smile to reassure her. She quickly glanced down, but he noted the slight tremor in her fingers as she took a bite of turkey and listened to his uncle with polite attention, a smile hovering on her mouth.

An image of her as a sixteen-year-old came to him. She'd faced the raw reality of life in those days with the same stoic candor. She hadn't danced, because no one had asked her; she'd made good grades because she'd had nothing to do but study, she'd told him.

But she'd had choices, he suddenly wanted to tell her. She could have been wild and defiant in the face of her parents' troubles. She could have skipped school, run away from home, become a drug addict. She hadn't done any of those things. Instead, she'd reached inside herself and taken her example from her grandparents, becoming a caring, responsible person.

He thought about his own life before he'd come to Lost Valley. Yes, he'd tried to redeem himself here at the ranch, but he knew the blackness that lived inside. It was the same as what lived within Frank Maguire. Seth was his father's son.

Amelia lived through the long family dinner, made it through dessert and coffee served in the living room. Just when she thought it would be okay to suggest she needed to get home, the baby, asleep in a bedroom, gave a cry.

Keith brought his son to Janis. The young mother murmured, ''Excuse me,'' and turned her back to the room while she nursed the infant.

The sounds of the suckling child did strange things to Amelia. First, her breasts hardened into visible beads against her sweater. She crossed her arms to disguise the fact. Second, her insides clenched into knots until she couldn't take a deep breath. She opened her mouth and inhaled carefully, feeling she was on the edge of breaking apart at any second.

She saw Seth's gaze go from Janis to her, then linger as she folded her arms over her breasts. He glanced up and met her eyes. For an eternity between one breath and the next, she couldn't look away.

The stark intensity of his gaze called to her, beckoning her into the dark world of their mutual desire. A drowning sensation rushed over her. She would find bliss in his arms, but then what?

She wanted more from him, she admitted. Her eyes were pulled to the mother and child. She looked back at him.

His expression didn't change, but his face seemed to harden into stony lines of denial.

She knew he was aware of the longing inside her, that she yearned for more than a brief relationship. She wanted love, marriage…a child. With him.

And for a second she thought his eyes were telling her he wanted the same. Then, without warning, he stood, excused himself and walked out of the house.

Silence ensued, followed by surprised gazes going from the door to her. She stared at her clasped hands.

"Wonder how the game is going," Uncle Nick said. "Zack, turn on the television. I believe it's the twins' turn to wash dishes."

Travis and Trevor voiced the expected protests, but went to the kitchen nevertheless. Alison volunteered to help. Janis finished feeding the baby and went to the bedroom with him.

Beau stood. "Would you like to go home now?" he asked, his eyes kind and concerned.

"Yes, please." She kissed Uncle Nick on the cheek. "Thank you so much for having me. It was a wonderful meal."

He raised troubled eyes to her and patted her shoulder. "Things have a way of coming right," he murmured.

She nodded and smiled, told everyone what a good time she'd had, and smiled, said goodbye and smiled….

Beau opened the door and held her arm to help

her out as if she were a fragile old lady. She felt that way.

''I'll take her home,'' Seth said, stepping between his truck and Beau's SUV. ''I'm going to town, anyway.''

Beau looked at her. ''Would you mind?''

She knew he wanted to stay with his wife and family. ''Of course not. Thank you for bringing me out.''

He nodded. To her surprise, he gave her a hug, then stepped aside, giving her room to go with Seth.

Without a word, Seth took her arm and guided her to the passenger side of his truck. He said goodbye to his brother and climbed in. Still silent, he drove away from the ranch and took the county road toward town.

''Did you enjoy the crowd?'' he finally asked.

''Yes.'' Her voice came out barely audible. She cleared her throat. ''Yes, it was a lovely dinner. My grandparents usually had a full house at Thanksgiving, too. I always loved it, everyone laughing and talking and eating. I used to entertain the little kids....''

She trailed off as memories formed a knot in her throat, reminding her of all the things she'd wished for as a child, the family she'd assumed she would have someday.

''What did you do?'' he asked.

She wondered if he was truly interested. ''Oh, we went for walks up to the lake and skipped stones, or collected pretty leaves to paste on construction paper,'' she said on a bright, false note.

''Don't,'' he said.

She licked her lips and tried to ignore the trembling inside. ''Don't what?''

''Don't be so damn brave!''

The words stunned her. ''I—I'm not,'' she stammered. ''I'm scared of snakes, spiders and odd-shaped shadows. And loud thunder.'' She tried to think of something else.

''And the devils of Seven Devils Ranch?'' he stated candidly. ''Or at least one of them.''

''You're not a devil.''

''Then what am I?''

His laughter was laced with mocking bitterness that she didn't like or understand. She sensed anger, perhaps despair, in him. But there was also longing—for what, she didn't know—and a hunger fathoms deep whenever he looked at her.

''My friend?'' she suggested gently. ''My lover?''

My love.

But she couldn't say that. His face went from angry to cold, as if ice enclosed his soul. Maybe it did. She looked out the window the rest of the way to town, watching the shadows deepen into twilight as they arrived home.

When they arrived at the B and B, she opened the door and started to exit the truck.

''Wait,'' he said.

He came around and lifted her in his arms, then

carried her into the house. Several guests welcomed her back when they went inside. The television was turned to a football game. One little boy slept in his mother's arms, another on the carpet at her feet. Caitlynn gave a quick wave as she refilled a cookie platter on the buffet.

Seth deposited Amelia on the sofa in her sitting room. "One of these days, Red, we'll have a long talk," he said. "Don't worry about Caitlynn. I'll drop her at her home before I go back to the ranch."

With that, he left.

Amelia puzzled over his words, then gave up trying to figure him out. She slipped off her shoes and the melted ice pack, then lifted her feet to the sofa and spread the chenille throw over her legs. Closing her eyes wearily, she admitted to feeling like a traveler who had come through a long and perilous journey and finally reached safety.

At the moment, she didn't want to see Seth Dalton again, much less have a long talk with him.

Then she laughed, because she knew she was lying, and because it was easier to laugh than to cry.

On Friday, Seth went to the office although he had no appointments for the day after Thanksgiving. Beau had a busy schedule at the medical clinic, he noted.

To Seth's surprise, four clients came by, needing advice on writing or updating their wills. That took care of the morning. At noon, Shelby invited him over for turkey salad sandwiches, cranberry sauce and pecan pie.

"Courtesy of Uncle Nick," she told him.

Nicky quietly took a seat at his side. "Hey, pal," Seth said to the boy. "Want to take a walk around the lake after lunch?"

"Yes, sir," Nicky said.

Seth's heart kicked around in his chest. He had a soft spot for children, he admitted. So did Amelia. Her whole being had been filled with longing while she observed Janis and her little one. He didn't think she'd realized it.

He forced his thoughts away from her and concentrated on finishing the meal. When he and Nicky were done, they grabbed their coats, said goodbye to Beau and Shelby and headed the few blocks to the lake.

Behind the lodge, they skipped stones over the smooth surface of the water. "Clouds over the peaks," Seth said.

Nicky studied the mountains. "Will we have a storm?"

"Maybe, although the mountains stop a lot of it from coming this way."

"I like the snow. It's pretty when it falls, and then it's fun to play in. Dad and Mom and I built a snowman last week. It melted, though."

Seth nodded. It was the first time he'd heard the boy refer to Shelby as his mother. Seth swallowed hard, knowing how important it was to children to have a settled life and a regular mom and dad like other kids.

He'd wanted the same thing at Nicky's age. He still did, except now he wanted to be the father. He wanted Amelia to be the woman in his life. Was that possible?

Frank's implied threats hung over his head, as ominous as the clouds over He-Devil Mountain. Seth could pay him off and make sure he got out of town by sending him a check care of general delivery in El Paso or someplace equally remote, so Frank would have to go there to pick it up.

"Uncle Seth? Are you sad?"

He focused on the boy. "Why do you ask that?"

Nicky shrugged. "My mom...my real mom... used to look sad sometimes. She was sad all the time before she went away. Are you going away?"

Seth lifted the five-year-old. Like him, Nicky knew the reality of his situation. That he had another mother out there somewhere and Shelby was sort of a borrowed one.

"No," he said, meaning it. "This is my home. My favorite people live here. I'm going to stay forever."

Nicky put his hands over his mouth and laughed. "Me, too," he confided, and hugged Seth's neck, his hands cold and damp from the stones.

Seth hugged the boy back. He realized he'd made a decision. Now all he had to do was carry it out.

* * *

The temporary phone, sitting on the floor where the check-in counter of the lodge would be, rang.

Seth noted the time. Almost noon. As usual on Saturdays, he'd started work that morning shortly after six, needing the activity and freedom from human company to think in peace. With a grimace, he slipped the hammer into the tool belt loop, laid the piece of window trim on the sill and went to answer the insistent caller.

"Hey, this is Zack," his cousin said. "I'm at the station. Uh, I have this guy here...says he wants to speak to you."

Seth frowned. A client? He was in no mood to handle some domestic disturbance case. "Who is it?"

"An older man, name of Frank Maguire. You know him?"

"Yes. What's the problem?"

"Well, shoplifting, I guess."

Seth cursed silently. It never paid to put off until tomorrow what one should have done yesterday. He'd thought he would have until Monday before he had to act.

"You guess? Don't you know?" he asked, injecting sardonic humor into the words.

"No. You'd better come on down."

"Be there in five minutes," Seth told him. He removed the tool belt, slapped the sawdust off his shirt and jeans, then headed for the police station, which was manned by contract with the sheriff's department.

Zack was at his desk when Seth arrived.

"Tell me what happened," Seth said, taking the chair beside the battered desk.

"Well, the hardware store owner says Maguire set off the alarm as he left the place. When we got there, we didn't find anything on him except part of an antishoplifting button, the type stores put on clothes and expensive items, in his coat pocket. He said it had been in the jacket since he bought it. He hadn't remembered to throw it away, but it had never set off an alarm before."

"Does the jacket look new?"

"No. It's been around the block a time or two."

"What about the store video? Did it show anything?"

"No one mentioned looking at it. Let's find out."

Seth rode with Zack to the hardware store. The two guys who owned it were married to Ruth, the midwife, and Bertie, the receptionist, at Beau's clinic. Small world. They all reviewed the video.

"Nothing," Seth said.

"I agree." Zack spoke to the owners about lack of evidence and the coincidence of the antishoplifting button.

"So why didn't it set the alarm off when he came in?" one of them inquired.

Zack shrugged. "Have you found anything missing?"

A digital camera was gone. They were checking inventory against cash register receipts, just in case it might have been sold and the transaction not recorded.

The suspect had been in custody from the moment he walked out of the store. There'd been no time for him to hide anything. "Without evidence, you don't have a case," the deputy told them.

They reluctantly agreed.

"Is he free to go?" Seth asked on the way back to the station.

"Yeah. We have no reason to hold him."

Seth waited in the outer room while Zack released the older man and returned his belongings. When Frank saw Seth, he smiled craftily. "I thought that would bring you out."

"Where's your truck?" Seth asked.

"At the fish camp. I don't have money for gas. If I did, I could get a job at the gas station on the highway."

Seth grunted skeptically and volunteered to drive the older man to the rented trailer. Parking behind the black pickup, he turned to Frank. "How much is it going to cost to get rid of you?" he asked.

He felt no emotion at buying out the man he'd once called Father. This was a business arrangement between two people who were basically strangers. He and his mother hadn't even used the Maguire name after the old man had gone to prison. Seth could almost see the wheels turning in Frank's head as he wondered how much he could squeeze out of his victim.

"Ten thousand," Frank at last said. "Just enough

to get a new start,'' he added, as if to justify the amount.

''I don't have that kind of money lying around. I'll have to arrange a loan from the bank.''

Frank snorted impatiently. ''You can get it from your rich uncle.''

A ripple spread over the dark pool within Seth. He stilled it and spoke calmly. ''Get real. He's a rancher. His assets are tied up in the land. Besides, I wouldn't ask him for a penny to give to you. I can get five thousand together in a couple of days, but that's it.''

Frank shook his head. ''I gotta have ten. I have a partner in Texas. We know where there's oil. You invest with us and you'll be rich,'' he said, with a con man's confidence in his schemes.

''No, thanks. I'm investing in my own future right here. The offer is now two thousand. Take it or leave it.''

Frank opened the vehicle door, his countenance mean, the way Seth remembered it from years ago. ''I'll think about it,'' he said, then got out and slammed the door behind him.

Seth backed up and turned around. For a while he drove aimlessly around the small town, which was bustling with Saturday traffic as ranchers and their wives came to town for shopping and a meal out. Without consciously planning to, he ended up at Amelia's home.

The pots of red poinsettias curved like welcoming arms on the front porch. The smoke from the chimney spoke of warmth inside. If he went in, she would ask him if he'd had lunch, then she would insist he stay and eat. The food would be filling, the company delightful.

He stared at the sturdy Victorian as the black pool of despair and anger and longing surged and rolled as if disturbed by a sudden storm.

Where can we go? he'd asked one night long ago.

The carriage house, she'd answered, her hands and mouth driving him wild with passion so strong, so deep, he'd never recovered from it.

But her answer, born of the moment and the wild elation that drove them to the brink, had been wrong.

Nowhere. That was the correct answer, the only answer as long as his past waited in ambush for him around each bend of life's road. By paying off the old man, Seth would be setting himself up for years of blackmail. Yesterday he'd decided to do just that. Today, confronted by the man's trickery—and he was sure the shoplifting incident was a ploy to bring him to his knees—he wasn't sure he could. There was only so much deceit a man could take or dish out.

He released the brake and set the truck in motion, passing the house where love and happiness lived. Until he solved the problem of Frank Maguire, until he figured out a way to silence all the lies he had ever spoken or implied by not speaking, he wasn't free to claim the heaven that his heart desired.

Chapter Twelve

Amelia woke with a start. She sat up in bed and listened intently, but heard nothing.

Maybe she'd been dreaming. Or perhaps one of her guests was restless and roaming the house. Looking at the clock, she realized it was the wee hours of Monday morning. The Thanksgiving weekend guests had left yesterday, with assurances that they had had a wonderful holiday and wanted to return next year.

The sound came again. Not a sharp noise, she realized, but the stirring of the wind through the house. The usual low, keening moan around the eaves lowered in pitch when one of the outside doors was opened. That change in sound was what had awakened her. Now it returned to its usual tone.

As if the door had been closed.

Goose bumps climbed her neck and tickled her scalp as she slipped out of bed and pulled on a robe and slippers. Silently, she lifted the portable phone and dialed the first two digits of 911 before making her way to the hall and peering toward the great room.

In the silence, she could hear only her heartbeat.

Taking a calming breath, she crept down the hallway. At the archway into the living room, she surveyed the premises. Nothing moved. She flicked on the light.

Her finger hovered over the *1* button on the phone, then she pressed it. The dispatcher answered at once. "Sheriff's office. Is this an emergency?"

"Uh, I think so. Someone broke into my house. This is Amelia Miller at the Lost Valley B and B."

"Is the intruder still in the house?"

The goose bumps attacked her neck again. "I don't think so. I don't see anyone. Some of my clocks are gone. And the silver service." She crossed to the office. "The cash box, too. It only had about fifty dollars in it."

"Please stay on the phone. An officer will be with you in a minute."

The dispatcher left the line, but returned almost at once to make sure Amelia was still there. "Stay where you are," he said. "Don't hang up."

"I won't." She wondered if they wanted to hear if the robber shot her or something. So they would have it on tape.

A few seconds later she heard an engine outside. Steps sounded on the wooden planks of the porch and the door was thrust open. She observed police procedure as the officer entered the house, gun drawn, and leaped to one side, his searching gaze taking in her and the entire room at a glance. He motioned for her to stay quiet.

She nodded.

Zack Dalton searched the rest of the downstairs area, then headed up the steps. Two more patrol cars arrived and four lawmen spilled out. They checked the grounds of the B and B and those of the house next door. To the east was a pasture.

Zack came down the steps from the second-floor guest rooms. ''All clear,'' he said.

''I think whoever it was left before I called,'' she said. ''That was what woke me up. The wind tone changed.''

He nodded as if this made perfect sense. ''Don't move,'' he ordered, and began a systematic examination of the room.

She surmised that he was searching for clues. For a moment it felt as if she'd stumbled onto the set of a TV movie in the making. Maybe she was the heroine of the show and didn't know it. She smiled with ironic humor. She didn't feel much like a heroine.

''Would it be okay to put on a pot of coffee?'' she asked. ''This might take a while.''

''Let me go first.''

Although he had already been through the kitchen, he led the way, Amelia at his heels. She started the coffeemaker while he withdrew a notebook from his pocket.

"Tell me everything that happened," he requested, taking a seat on a stool.

She explained about waking up to the change in pitch of the wind around the house.

"That's all?" he asked. "You didn't see anyone leave or hear a car start up outside?"

She shook her head.

"We'll dust for fingerprints." He didn't sound as if he expected to find any.

One of the deputies came in. "We found this."

"That's my cash box," she told them.

"Check it for prints," Zack ordered. "Where was it?"

"Under a tree by the side of the house."

"He came in by that door," Amelia said. "I can tell when it's opened because it makes a draft in the chimney in my quarters. That's what causes the wind to shift notes as it blows around the eaves. It woke me up."

"Let's check the door," Zack told the other deputy.

She followed the two men to the east wing. They examined the door, using the beam from a flashlight.

"Scrape marks," the deputy said.

"Yeah," Zack agreed. "He probably used a screwdriver to force the bolt. The frame is cracked here."

She frowned at the long splinter of wood hanging loose from the frame. The thief had broken her door, a fact that upset her more than the actual robbery. A person's home was sacrosanct. No one should enter without an invitation.

Yeah, right.

"Are you okay?"

Amelia nodded in answer to Zack's question.

"I didn't see anyone in the rooms. Are you alone here tonight?"

"Yes."

He glanced at his watch. "I go off duty in an hour. I can stay. Is my old room vacant?"

"Yes, but you don't have to baby-sit me. I'm sure I'll be okay." She smiled a trifle weakly. "Surely thieves don't strike the same place twice in one night."

He patted her shoulder. "Not likely, but that door won't lock until it's repaired. Seth would have my hide if I left you without protection."

His grin was meant to be reassuring as well as joking. Heat swept into her face, but at the same time a shiver rushed over her. She realized they were standing with the door wide open. The furnace was on, but it couldn't heat the whole outdoors.

"I'll nail the door closed," she said.

"Good idea." Zack turned to the other deputy. "Let's see if there's anything else outside."

Amelia returned to the kitchen, where she set her toolbox on the counter and found several nails in the catch-all drawer. Then she set out a platter of muffins for the lawmen, plus cups and the creamer and sugar bowl.

An hour later, the five lawmen yawned, finished the last of the muffins and pumpkin bread, gathered their stuff and left, after making sure the side door, secured with three nails, couldn't be opened.

Amelia cleared the kitchen, refreshed her tea and headed for her sitting room. It was 5:00 a.m. and sleep was far from her mind.

She'd hardly gotten settled before the front doorbell rang. Startled, she hurried to see what the deputies had forgotten. Her hand flew to her throat when she recognized who stood on the doorstep.

"What are you doing here?" she asked.

Seth stepped inside. He glanced around the room. "Zack called. He said you'd had a break-in."

She nodded. "Everything is taken care of. I'm having a cup of tea. You want some?"

"I'll fix it. You go rest."

Rolling her eyes at his take-charge manner, she went back to the sitting room and turned on the gas logs. Seth joined her a couple of minutes later with a cup of tea. He settled on the sofa and let out an audible breath.

"Tell me what happened," he said.

She repeated her story.

His face was grim when she finished. Anger, so cold and intense it frightened her, exuded from his powerful body.

"Have you seen anyone suspicious around here?" he asked, his tone curiously soft.

"No." She reconsidered. "There was a man."

"What did he look like?"

She raised troubled eyes to his. ''An older man, sort of scruffy looking. He came to your office that day when Shelby and I were arranging the furniture.''

Seth's hands tightened on the cup, but he said nothing.

''He asked for you,'' she continued. ''Later I saw him in a pickup truck parked on the side of the street. Then he came here—''

''When?'' Seth interrupted.

''The day I went for a walk by the lake and saw you at the lodge. He was inside when I returned.''

An odd expression crossed Seth's face. ''I walked you home but didn't come in. I didn't think....''

His voice trailed off as he lapsed into deep, dark thoughts. Amelia studied him, unable to figure out the turbulent emotions she sensed in him.

Could it mean he did care, after all?

Suddenly he rose and started toward the door.

''Where are you going?'' she asked, startled by his conduct.

''To see a man about a dog,'' he answered shortly.

She sighed as the tiny, forlorn hope evaporated. Hearts, it seemed, were stubborn about giving up, but it was time hers learned to do so.

Seth parked on the side of the gravel lane that snaked in a loop through the fishing resort. The black pickup was parked beside the trailer. He noted that the hookup lines to water and electricity were still in place.

He checked out the truck first. Seeing nothing of interest, he went to the trailer door and knocked softly, not out of consideration for the occupant but because he didn't intend to call attention to the visit. He wanted it to be quiet and quick.

The door opened. "Well, well, well," Frank Maguire muttered, stepping back as Seth came inside.

"Where are they?" Seth asked.

Frank gave him a guileless look. "Where are what?"

"The things you stole when you broke into the B and B early this morning." Seth started opening drawers and cabinets.

"Hey, what the hell do you think you're doing?" the old man demanded. "That's my stuff."

Other than cooking and eating utensils, the cabinets and storage compartments were empty of personal effects. Seth checked the bathroom and closet that formed a partition between the living and sleeping compartments.

In a grocery bag in the bedroom, he found what he was looking for—three old-fashioned enameled clocks and a silver teapot with matching creamer and sugar bowl. He returned to the other room with the items.

"I suppose you're going to turn me in to your deputy cousin?" Frank sneered. "Wonder what he'll think when he learns I'm your long lost dad?"

''Any fool can sire a child,'' Seth said. ''It takes a man to be a father. You were never that.''

He observed the rage in Frank's face, then the flash of cunning in the old man's eyes. Seth's own fury dissipated, and he felt only a vague weariness at the sorry life represented by the man before him. Other than that, he felt nothing toward this stranger—neither anger nor hatred nor fear.

''A man learns a thing or two in prison,'' Frank said.

''Such as?'' Seth asked, not really interested.

''Well now, as I understand it, a lawyer is an officer of the court. What happens to one who lies or goes by a false name? Does he lose his license?''

Seth shrugged. ''Why don't you go to the bar association and find out?''

''Maybe I will. Don't think I'm scared to do it,'' Frank warned, his expression threatening and scornful.

Seth couldn't help comparing this pitiful wreck of a human with Uncle Nick, the one so vile, the other so good.

''It doesn't matter what you do,'' he said. ''You beat us when I was a kid. You didn't care whether Mom and I starved or froze. It takes a long time for a kid's trust to die, but it finally does. Do you really think I'm going to give in to blackmail?''

''I didn't say anything about blackmail,'' Frank said, reverting to a whine. ''A man needs a grubstake, naturally he comes to his own family.''

Seth ignored the reference to kinship. ''Speaking

of money, there's a little matter of the fifty dollars you stole from the cash box. Where is it?''

''I don't know what you're talking about.''

''Hand it over,'' Seth ordered, ''or we can call the cops and turn over this stuff.'' He gestured toward the bag of stolen goods.

Frank hesitated long enough that Seth knew the man was figuring the odds on whether he was bluffing. Seth gave him a wolfish smile, almost wishing he would take the challenge. After a full minute, Frank pulled out a wallet and tossed it on the table.

Seth took the cash out and counted it. He tossed a twenty dollar bill and a couple of ones on the laminated counter, along with the wallet, and stuffed Amelia's money in his pocket. He drew out his own wallet and threw down an additional five hundred dollars. Frank's eyes lit up.

''That's it,'' Seth said. ''Enough to get you out of town and on your way south before the weather turns really nasty.''

Frank picked up the money with a satisfied gleam. ''I knew you wouldn't let me down. It ain't natural for a son to turn away from his father.''

Seth paused at the door. He doubted Frank would understand, but he said, ''The money is yours, but you're not the reason behind it. Consider it a gift from Camilla, the woman who loved you and believed in your dreams. She told me she once truly thought we would have a ranch of our own. If we all worked hard. If we pulled together. Then she realized you didn't want to work for it—you wanted someone to hand it to you. People make choices in life. You deserted your wife, your son and those dreams. You lost it all, old man.''

''Things were against me. It was too much—''

Seth cut him off, slicing his hand through the air. ''No excuses. You broke her heart and I'll never forgive you for that.'' He stopped, then added softly, ''She's gone, so there's nothing more you can do to hurt her. Or me. If you're wise, you'll leave the state and make a new, decent life somewhere. As an officer of the court, I'll turn you in if you try to steal anything else or make any more threats around here. That's a promise.''

He gazed into Frank's eyes without blinking as he delivered the simple truth. The old man returned his stare with a narrow-eyed, resentful gaze, then looked away. He stuffed the bills into his wallet and pocketed it.

Seth realized there was nothing more to be said between them. He stepped outside and silently closed the door.

The sun was fully up now. The interior of the truck was warm. He realized he'd left the B and B without his coat. Feeling a curious numbness, he returned to the comfortable house and went inside. The front door was unlocked. As usual.

''Seth?'' Amelia called.

''Yeah, it's me.''

She appeared at the Dutch door to the kitchen, looking distraught. ''I need your help. Someone dropped some kittens by the carriage house driveway. Two of them died—from exposure, I suppose—but the third is still alive. I'm trying to feed it. Poor thing. It's so weak.''

He set the stolen items on the floor and went to her. In a box lined with towels, a tiny kitten, its eyes barely open, mewed plaintively, the sound so weak he could hardly hear it.

Amelia dipped her finger in a bowl of milk and tried to get the kitten to lick. It didn't raise its head.

''It's too small to make it,'' he told her.

''I can't just let it die.''

She looked up at him, her eyes so filled with distress that he had to crush an urge to take her into his arms. ''Okay, let me think.'' He had an idea. ''I'll be back in a minute,'' he told her. ''I know where we can get some help.''

He drove to the clinic and hurried inside. ''Shelby, I need some supplies. Amelia found a baby kitten, apparently abandoned, and is trying to feed it. It's too weak to drink but I think we may be able to squirt the milk down its throat. A syringe with no needle should do the trick. You got one I can use?''

''I think so.''

She showed him different sizes. He chose the largest. ''This might do it.''

''Mmm, cow's milk could be too rich.'' She opened a cabinet and removed a can of formula. ''Here, take this and see if the kitten can tolerate it. Wait. I have a couple of milk pouches. I'll find something to put them in.''

From the refrigerator, she selected four plastic containers filled with formula, and put them in a bag with a plastic bottle, after showing him how they worked. She added the canned formula to the package. "Use the syringe with the canned formula first. The kitten may be seriously dehydrated. You need to get liquids down it as quickly as possible."

"Thanks." He headed out.

At the B and B, he hurried to the kitchen. Amelia held the kitten in one arm and was dripping milk into its mouth with her finger. Most of the milk dribbled onto her blouse as the tiny creature licked feebly.

Seth knelt beside her. "Here, perhaps this will help."

After filling the syringe with canned milk, he gently opened the tiny mouth and inserted the tip. Having no idea how much the kitten could swallow, he pushed the plunger a tiny bit. Milk bubbled over the pink gums and down his hand, then he felt the kitten swallow. He squirted a little more. It swallowed again.

Amelia smiled at him, her eyes brilliant with gratitude and hope. His insides unraveled.

"I think that will work," he said huskily, and let her take the syringe.

She laughed as the kitten bobbed its head around until it found the end of the tube, then latched on. To his surprise, it started sucking. Amelia crooned in pleasure and slowly fed it the formula. Twenty minutes later, the kitten lay snug in the box, its black-and-white furred tummy puffed out like a miniature soccer ball.

"Thank you," Amelia whispered.

Her lips were only inches from Seth's as they sat on the floor beside the box. The temptation was too much. He bent his head, then kissed her before all the reasons he shouldn't drummed through him.

He traced her lips with his tongue, experienced their soft warmth with his own, felt her sigh as she leaned forward. He ended the kiss reluctantly.

"Let's take Pele to the sitting room. I'll turn on the gas fire."

"Pele?"

"That's the only famous soccer player I know," she said, touching the rounded tummy with its black and white splotches.

"Is it a him?"

"Yes." She gave Seth a mischievous glance. "I checked while you were gone. I suppose we have Beau to thank for the supplies?"

"Shelby, actually. I thought of the syringe, but she added the formula and other stuff." He helped Amelia to her feet and picked up the box with the sleeping kitten.

In the great room, he spotted the other bag he'd brought in earlier. Once the kitten was snug near the warm hearth, Seth handed the grocery bag to Amelia. "This belongs to you."

She peeked in the bag cautiously. Her mouth dropped open when she saw the contents. "Where did you get these?" she asked, plainly bewildered.

He reached into his pocket and withdrew the fifty dollars. He dropped the bills in her lap. "I found the man who took them."

"The older man with the black pickup?"

Seth nodded, not surprised that she correctly connected the dots of the mystery so fast.

She frowned. "But how did you know… I mean, why him? Because he was the only stranger to come here?" Her eyes opened wider. "He came to your office first. Maybe he was going to rob you and Beau."

Seth laid a finger over her lips and lingered to caress that delectable temptation.

She took his hand in hers and kissed the back before pressing his palm to her cheek. "Do you know him? Was he a client of yours?"

He shook his head, then sat beside her on the sofa. "Later," he murmured, unable to tear his gaze from her mouth. "I'll tell you later."

"When?" She caressed his jaw and pushed her fingers into his hair, her eyes sexily warm and passionate.

He knew he couldn't take all she offered. Not yet. "There's someone I have to talk to first."

She studied him, then said, "Uncle Nick?"

Seth nodded. Cupping her face, he claimed her lips, drinking in her innocence, the honey of her passion, as she responded without hesitation. Maybe it was foolish to do this, to take this much, knowing he could be left with nothing when he told the two people who mattered most to him the sordid story of his past.

He held her tighter, as if some evil spirit would snatch her right out of his arms if he didn't keep his guard up. "You'd better tell me to go, Red," he said hoarsely.

He felt her sigh against his chest. She leaned her head against him for a moment. "Go," she replied softly. "When you can come to me with gladness in your heart, then..."

Rising, he gazed at her averted face and knew the moment he'd always dreaded had arrived. "Let's go to the ranch," he said, making the decision and knowing she had to be included. "Will you come?"

She hesitated, then nodded.

He checked his watch. Seven. Uncle Nick would be up and dressed.

Just then a ray of sunshine broke through the early morning clouds, coating the landscape in light. The brightness seemed to enter Seth's soul. Whatever happened after this, he would at last be free of subterfuge and deceit. That, at least, was something to look forward to.

"Seth?"

"What is it, Red?" He couldn't keep the huskiness from his voice.

"Whatever it is, it won't matter," she said firmly.

He'd always known she had courage. "Maybe," he said, managing a smile for her. "Maybe not."

Chapter Thirteen

Seth reviewed the vehicles parked around the quadrangle between the ranch house, barns and fences. Zack's patrol SUV was there. He was probably sleeping after working a double shift the previous night. The station wagon was missing, so Trevor was probably in town.

Honey came out the door just as he parked. ''Hi,'' she called when he and Amelia crossed the lawn. ''Uncle Nick's inside. Zack's asleep. Everyone else is out. I'm heading in for my nine o'clock class.''

''We came to see Uncle Nick,'' Seth told her.

Questions leaped into her eyes, but she nodded, smiled at them and went on her way. Seth was grateful for small favors. He led the way inside.

Uncle Nick had the TV on a news channel. He turned it off upon their entrance. "Seth, Amelia," he said. "Come into the kitchen. I'll make fresh coffee."

"Thanks. That would be great." Seth hung up his and Amelia's coats. They joined the older man at the kitchen table a minute later.

"Cold this morning," Uncle Nick said. He finished with the coffeemaker, asked if they would like some doughnuts, which they declined, then sat down at the table.

"It's supposed to snow later this week," Amelia commented. "I hope so. We need the snowpack in the mountains for water next summer."

"True." Uncle Nick studied Seth, then asked, "What do you think?"

Seth hadn't really been listening to the small talk, but some part of his mind had followed it. "Yeah, we need the snow."

He glanced from the older man's shrewd, level gaze to Amelia's composed expression. She'd clasped her hands on the table and sat almost statue still as she waited for his news. Light from the kitchen window, shining behind her, turned her hair to glowing embers, a halo of warmth.

He took a deep breath and began. "There are things I think you should know. Both of you. All of the Daltons, actually."

"Let's not worry about the rest of the family yet," Uncle Nick suggested.

Seth nodded. "I'll start at the beginning. Twenty-two years ago, my mom was asked to baby-sit several kids during the rodeo. Those kids belonged to Job and Jed Dalton, twins who toured the rodeo circuit together. Job's wife was dead. Jed's wanted to attend the rodeo events without keeping track of five kids.''

He glanced at Amelia to make sure she was following the tale. She knew most of it due to the grapevine, and he had never denied how he came to be with the Dalton brothers. The coffeemaker finished perking. He rose, poured them each a cup and returned to the table.

''Mom and I were in California at the time, but originally we came from Nevada. We never lived in Idaho. We never even visited here.'' He paused and looked at the Dalton patriarch. ''Until we came north with Job Dalton.''

Uncle Nick nodded.

Seth stared at the cheerful striped cloth covering the table, recalling those early years and the excitement of being with the Dalton men and their families.

''A new life,'' his mom had promised, her eyes shining.

It had been a few more years before he'd been old enough to realize she'd fallen in love with Job. Fortunately, the feeling had been mutual, and the twin had wanted them to come north and meet the oldest brother of the Dalton clan and see the ranch.

Seth's throat tightened as he remembered how

happy she'd been. It was the first true joy he'd ever seen in her.

"Then the avalanche happened. Job and Jed were suddenly gone, along with Jed's wife and my mother." He glanced at Amelia. "All her dreams were for nothing."

Her eyes filled with pity. He looked away.

"But there was hope at the end of that tragedy. Uncle Nick and Aunt Milly."

"We were glad to have you," the older man said.

Seth continued, determined to get to the bitter end of the tale. "When asked about my relatives and where I was from, I said I didn't know." The next words were hard, so hard to say to this man who taught truth and kindness by example. "I lied."

His snort of laughter was meant to be ironic, but it sounded hollow to his ears.

"What kid wouldn't?" he continued doggedly, wanting to get everything in the open. "With a ranch to roam and horses to ride, with plenty of food and a passel of kids to romp with, what twelve-year-old would give that up willingly?"

Uncle Nick's chuckle was genuinely amused. "They used to play cowboys and Indians," he said to Amelia. "Seth always had to be the Indian. Did you mind?" he asked, turning to him.

Zack surprised them when he appeared from the bedroom wing. "Why should he? He always won." He covered a yawn. "Is this a private party, or can anyone join?"

Seth gestured toward a chair. "Take a seat."

After Zack grabbed a cup of coffee, he joined the other three at the table.

"I lied because I wanted to stay here, but I knew exactly where my father was." Seth took a drink of coffee to ease the tightness in his throat. "In prison."

Seth was acutely aware of the eyes on him, all of them shades of blue, a sharp contrast to his own dark ones. He was the misfit, he acknowledged grimly, the ugly duckling who was never meant to be a swan.

Zack frowned as if puzzled, but he remained silent. When Seth looked at him, he motioned for him to continue.

"Frank Maguire was his name," Seth said.

Zack's hand jerked, spilling the coffee.

Seth handed him a napkin and went on. "Frank had a mean streak. He killed a man in a brawl and was sentenced to prison for manslaughter. He had a brother, just as mean and hot-tempered. My mom had no close relatives, but I knew where my uncle lived. I didn't want to go to him, so I pretended I didn't remember where I was born or where we came from."

"Ah," Uncle Nick said, nodding as if he understood completely. "Old Doc Barony thought the shock of losing your mother had caused you to lose your memory."

"I didn't want to lie to you," Seth admitted, "so I said as little as possible."

"But you knew and that knowledge bothered you."

His kind voice held not one trace of censure. Seth fought the turmoil of emotion that filled his chest, and nodded. "I vowed you would never regret letting me stay. When you lied for me and said I was your brother's son, I promised on my mother's grave that I'd be the best person there ever was and that I would never give you and Aunt Milly reason to regret the day you took me in."

"We never did," Uncle Nick said softly. "Milly and I were proud of you, of all our children."

Pain seared like a branding iron in Seth's chest. "Aunt Milly died and Tink disappeared, but still you kept us all. I learned ranching and tried to earn my keep. I found out about honor and integrity and that a man's word is the most sacred thing he has. I learned from a man who displayed all those qualities." He looked at Uncle Nick.

"No, son," the old man said huskily, "you had all those qualities in you."

Seth shook his head. "I had a police record behind me. Twelve years old and I'd been in trouble with the law most of my life."

He saw the shock ripple across Amelia's face and felt an answering stab in his heart as she learned the truth about him and his life.

"For what?" Zack asked.

"Stealing, mostly. When I was seven, I tried to shoplift a scarf from a store."

Amelia spoke for the first time since he'd started the great confession. "For your mother."

There was no question in her voice, no condemnation in her eyes. He would have loved her for that alone if he hadn't already loved her for so many other things.

The wonder of that love drew a rainbow across his inner vision, a promise of all the things a man could dream of. With that wonder came an ache to add to the others in his life. Would she love him at the end of this day?

"That time," he admitted. "Later..." He shrugged. "It was for kicks or maybe revenge on a society that didn't seem to give a damn about us. For the next few years, I watched the life drain out of my mother. We had tried to get away from my father several times, but he wouldn't leave us alone. He always found us. When I was ten, he went to prison and she and I got out of the state. It was a chance to go someplace where he couldn't find us, and start a new life. We used my grandmother's maiden name, calling ourselves Camilla White Feather Diego and Seth Diego. So that was a lie, too. My real name was Seth Maguire."

"Is that when you moved to California?" Zack asked.

"We traveled all over the Southwest as migrant workers." He laughed without humor. "We nearly starved, but Mom said we were on a great adventure. Slowly we started putting our lives back together.

California was nice because it wasn't so cold when we slept in the car."

He saw Amelia blink back tears, and longed to bury his face in her hair and hold her, just hold her.

"Anyway, time passed," he said, needing to finish. "Things got better. Then someone asked about a baby-sitter and was referred to us. Mom and I took any job we could get. I entertained the five Dalton kids until she was done waiting tables in a tent at the rodeo grounds. We did that for ten days. Job Dalton asked us to go with him to the next rodeo and help with his kids. We talked it over and agreed. We spent the whole summer and fall with the Daltons. By then, things were serious between Job and my mother." Seth took a deep breath. "And that's how we came here."

Amelia couldn't have spoken if her life depended on it when he finished his tale. She saw so much more than he said—the brutality inflicted by the man who was his father, the worry and desperation of a child who wanted to protect his mother, the hope kindled when Job Dalton had asked them to join him.

"So Uncle Job wasn't your father," Zack said, putting the pieces together.

"No," Seth affirmed. "I prayed he would marry my mom, but I'm not sure it would have been legal. I'm not positive she was divorced from Frank. After we started our new life, we never spoke of him again. It was like he didn't exist."

Amelia forced back tears. Instinctively, she knew there was more.

"But I knew he did. I always knew." Seth finished his story in a voice so devoid of emotion it was as if a part of him had died during the telling.

His eyes, when he looked at the elder Dalton, were pools of darkness. Amelia longed to go to him, to comfort that boy who had so wanted a home and who'd felt guilty all his life for taking his heart's desire when it was offered. But some inner wisdom said Seth wasn't ready for that.

Uncle Nick sat in quiet contemplation for a long minute. Finally he leaned forward and laid his hand on Seth's arm. "My brother told me, the very morning of the day he was killed, that he and Camilla were going to marry. He said he was going to adopt you."

Amelia glanced at Seth. She saw his throat move as he swallowed. It was a moment before he spoke. "I've lied about everything," he said. "My whole life has revolved around that. I let you believe I might be your brother's son when I knew I wasn't. I let you lie for me."

"Job told me you had the makings of a fine man," Uncle Nick said sternly. "I didn't know you then, but I trusted my brother's judgment. You've proved he spoke the truth."

He sat back in the chair, reminding Amelia of a man who's said all he intends to on the subject. She studied Seth, trying to discern how he took this news. When he stood, she knew he wasn't convinced.

"Tell them," he said now to Zack. "Tell them who's in town. Maybe then they'll understand all this."

She and Uncle Nick turned to Zack.

He explained about Frank Maguire being in town. "I think I have it figured out," he said, his eyes on Seth. "I think Maguire is trying to squeeze money out of you. If he succeeds, you'll never know a moment's peace again."

"Don't you think I know that?" Seth paced the room. "I did give him enough money to get out of town. But he knows it's the last he'll get from me."

He paused, then lifted his hands and stared at them with such bleak despair it caused a chill to sweep over Amelia.

"There's more," Seth said in a low, weary tone. "Frank was waiting for me one night outside your house," he said, glancing at Amelia. "He wanted money. When he made his demand and threatened to expose me as his son, I wanted…I wanted to kill him."

Silence pounded through the room like a heartbeat gone wild as Seth rammed his hands into his pockets and paced again.

Slowly Uncle Nick nodded, then asked softly, "Did you kill him?"

Seth shook his head impatiently. "But I wanted to. Don't you understand? I wanted to strangle him with my bare hands. I wanted to take a rock and beat the sneer off his face. I wanted him out of my life—this stolen life that I have no right to—and I wanted him gone forever.''

Nicholas Dalton stood. Amelia knew then why other men respected him. Like a prophet from biblical days, the older man seemed filled with power, a power even more forceful because it was so carefully controlled.

''Did you kill him?'' he repeated levelly.

The two men stared each other in the eye.

''Don't you think I wanted to kill the man who may have caused the wreck that killed my wife, who stole my child for God knows what purposes?'' Uncle Nick continued. ''Don't you think I've envisioned a thousand tortures to visit upon that man before I let him die?''

Tension blanketed the room in black cobwebs, binding them all into this strange tableau of pain and guilt and despair. Amelia shivered uncontrollably.

''That even now,'' the older man said softly, ''I sometimes wish him a painful death. But I know I wouldn't do it…for the same reasons you didn't harm Frank Maguire. You're a Dalton, and Daltons are honorable men.''

''I'm not—''

''You are,'' Nicholas interrupted. He smote his chest with a fist. ''In here, where it counts, you are one of us. If it's a question of legality, we can fix that. I'll adopt you.''

The muscles in Seth's jaw clenched. The strong planes of his face hardened until he appeared savage, untamed and removed from all that was civilized. Without a word, he walked out of the house and drove away.

Amelia felt they would never see him again, that he would disappear into the wilderness surrounding the Seven Devils Mountains and become one with the land, a wild creature who shunned mankind. She wanted to lay her head on the table and let her grief out in long, keening wails—like a she-wolf who had lost her mate.

Uncle Nick sighed. ''I always hated to punish Seth when he was little. He was so much harder on himself than I could ever be. Now I understand the burden he carried inside. It would have broken a grown man, and he was only a boy.''

Caught up in the turbulence of her own childhood, Amelia had never realized Seth's pain all those years ago. He'd been one of the Dalton gang, confident and assured. Or so she'd thought back then.

Walk a mile in another's shoes, her grandmother had always said.

''The appearance of his father isn't the only reason he told us the truth.'' Nicholas looked at Amelia. ''I knew he'd been troubled about something the past couple of months. He has feelings for you, but he couldn't give in to them because of the past. He couldn't live a lie with you.''

''His past doesn't matter to me,'' she protested.

''It does to him,'' the older man said.

''What do we do now?'' Zack asked.

Uncle Nick thought it over. ''We'll tell the rest

of the family, then we'll wait for Seth to come home.''

Zack looked dubious. ''You think he will?''

The family patriarch nodded. ''When he forgives himself. When he realizes a man can't live without his family or the woman of his dreams. I believe he's loved you for a long time, girl. Do you feel the same?''

Amelia nodded, her heart knocking with hope and with fear. ''Since we were in high school,'' she said.

''Well, then, we wait.''

Christmas was only two days away. The fir tree in the great room was decorated in red and gold and made the B and B smell deliciously outdoorsy. Amelia glanced at the calendar in her office, finished the reservation form on the computer and printed out two copies—one for her files and one to mail to the clients as a confirmation.

She tucked the portable phone in her pocket as she went about her chores. After cleaning the last guest room, she stored the vacuum and supplies in the upstairs closet. The six second-floor bedrooms had been full over the weekend, a surprise, since she'd only had two rooms booked. The others had been taken by chance visitors to the area.

She hadn't seen Seth since Zack had driven her home from the ranch after Seth had told them about his past. The kitten had greeted her return with an almost inaudible mewing demand to be fed again. Its care helped her concentrate on the present rather than the past and her fear that Seth would leave the area and never come back. Ignoring the pain in her heart, she went to the great room and started a fire in the large grate.

No one was due in now for almost two weeks. She always reserved the week between Christmas and the New Year for private time. Hearing a car door slam outside, she smiled and headed in that direction. She was expecting her parents.

Peering out one of the leaded glass panels, she saw it was them. She went out to help with their luggage.

"Mom! Dad! You're here!" she called in welcome.

"I hope you have something warm to drink," her father said, returning her hug. "It's colder than a Klondike gold digger's you-know-what around here."

"We had fresh snow yesterday and more is forecast for tomorrow. I love snow for Christmas."

"You would," her mother teased ruefully. As usual, she was dressed stylishly in a red pantsuit with a striped top, her hair in natural-looking blond curls around her oval face. Her earrings were tiny sparkling Christmas trees. "I can't wait for your father to retire. We're moving someplace where they never have snow."

Inside, Amelia led the way to the large room in the east wing and helped her parents store their things in the spacious armoire.

"Are we sharing the bath?" her mother asked.

"No. You're my only guests for the holidays. Come to the sitting room when you're ready. I want you to meet the latest addition to the family."

At her mother's startled glance, which fell quickly to her bare ring finger, Amelia realized how her words could be taken. "It's a kitten," she added quickly, and left her parents to freshen up while she prepared hot buttered rum, her father's favorite cold weather tipple, and hot tea with a tablespoon of Irish cream liqueur, her mom's choice.

With determined cheerfulness, Amelia set about making the evening a pleasant one. Her mother exclaimed over the kitten, which played about the room until tired, then curled into a ball in her mom's lap.

"Sing us a song," her father requested.

Amelia got out her guitar and sang a couple of ballads, then she played while her parents harmonized on some carols, their voices blending beautifully, which struck her as an irony when compared to their turbulent lives.

"Guess what?" her mom said just before they went off to bed. "Your father and I stopped in Reno on the way here."

Amelia didn't get the connection.

"We got married," her father said. "Again. This time we think it'll work."

"Oh," she said blankly, then exclaimed, "Oh, that's wonderful! Congratulations!"

They talked for another hour about the couple's plans to retire next year and go on a world cruise.

"Or something equally extravagant, while we're still young enough to enjoy it," her mom told her. Giving her husband a wicked glance, she added, "And I can still flirt with all the young studs hired to pamper us."

Amelia quickly glanced at her father. His smile was easy. She relaxed. Her parents had learned to accept each other. After they said good-night, she sat in front of the fire with the kitten snoozing beside her. She'd never felt so lonely. At midnight, she went to bed.

Amelia woke and checked the time. Five o'clock. While she normally rose at five-thirty, this was Christmas Eve, for heaven's sake. She could sleep in.

After ten minutes of keeping her eyes closed, she sighed, tossed the covers off and headed for the shower. Twenty minutes later she stifled a yawn as she entered the sitting room. Then she stopped dead still.

Feet dangled over the end of the sofa. Her father? Had her parents had a quarrel after going to their room?

With silent footsteps, she approached the sofa and peered over the back. There, the kitten sleeping snugly against his neck and shoulder, was Seth.

He opened his eyes and looked up at her. "Hi."

"Where have you been?" she blurted in shock, then wished she could recall the words, which revealed her worry of the past three weeks.

"In Boise, checking on things." He lifted the kitten, rose and replaced the round ball of fur on the pillow. "It seems the lawyer Uncle Nick used all those years ago filed a formal change of name for me. Uncle Nick won't have to adopt me, after all."

She couldn't think of anything to say. "Well, that's good. Isn't it?"

He smiled. His hair looked delightfully tousled and his eyes tantalizingly sexy.

A hot surge of need poured through her. "How did you get in?" she asked.

"The side door. Zack said you'd had it repaired. I hope you don't mind that I used the key you gave me."

"Uh, no. The single room was available." She glanced at the sofa and back at him. "How long have you been here?"

"I got in from the city around two this morning. I wanted to see you first thing, so I slept in here."

"Oh." She started for the kitchen. "I'll put some coffee on. We can have breakfast."

He caught her wrist. "I have something for you." He pointed to the small tree on the side table.

A white box was balanced in its branches. Her eyes flew to his, while her feet remained rooted to the spot.

He retrieved the box. "I talked to Uncle Nick yesterday," he said huskily. "He thinks..." Seth shook his head, frowned, then smiled a trifle wryly. "I'll start over. There are things in my past that I can't change."

"Your past doesn't bother me," she quickly said.

"Fair enough. There are things in my future I'd like to change." He opened the white satin box and removed a ring. "I didn't think I had a right to ask a woman to take a name I wasn't sure I was entitled to, but…"

Eons passed and she died a thousand deaths as she waited for him to finish.

"But now I know the Dalton name is mine to give. Will you marry me, Red? I'll try to be the best husband you could ever want. Uncle Nick said he would help keep me straight. So did the rest of the gang."

His grin was playful, but his eyes…oh, his eyes!

"Yes," she said. "Of course. I…there's never been anyone but you." Should she have admitted that much? She gazed at him anxiously.

He put the ring on her finger. "It was the same for me. Since the night I walked a girl home from a dance and kissed her until the stars fell down around us, I've never been able to look at another that way. I love you more than anything, more than life itself."

"Kiss me," she whispered, moving into his embrace when his arms closed around her. "I think the stars are starting to fall."

"Again," he said.

The kiss was all it had been those many years ago, carrying the promise of the future in the growing tide of passion between them. When they grew weak from the force of it, they fell to the sofa.

A startled ''meow'' interrupted them.

Chuckling, Seth moved the kitten to a safe place on the rocking chair. Amelia noticed the gentleness of his touch and the affectionate undertone as he assured the little one they would be more careful in the future.

''What?'' he asked, seeing the mist film her eyes.

''You'll be a wonderful father to our children,'' she told him, choked with love for him, this man who held her heart in his strong, gentle hands.

''I'll try,'' he promised with all the heartfelt earnestness born of a boy's dream and a man's word. ''For you, Red. Anything for you.''

That was good enough.

* * * * *

The lone female devil is next on Uncle Nick's parade, but who is he going to tell her to seduce? The SEVEN DEVILS *saga continues with Roni...and someone you've met before...coming to Special Edition in Fall 2003!*

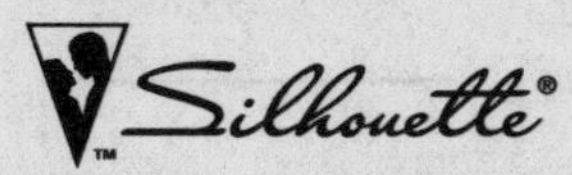

SPECIAL EDITION®

COMING NEXT MONTH

#1561 HARD CHOICES—Allison Leigh
Readers' Ring
A night of passion long ago had resulted in a teenage pregnancy—specifically, the fifteen-year-old who now stood on Annie Hess's doorstep. Now, reformed wild child Annie was forced to confront her past…and Logan Drake, the man who had unknowingly fathered her child.

#1562 A WINCHESTER HOMECOMING—Pamela Toth
Winchester Brides
Kim Winchester returned home after a bitter divorce to find peace—not to face even more emotional turmoil. Seeing rancher and former childhood sweetheart David Major stirred up feelings in her that she'd rather not deal with…feelings that David wouldn't let her ignore….

#1563 BIG SKY BABY—Judy Duarte
Montana Mavericks: The Kingsleys
Pregnant and alone, Jilly Davis knew there was only one man she could turn to—her best friend, Jeff Forsythe. She needed his strong, dependable shoulder to lean on, but what she found in his arms was an attraction she couldn't deny!

#1564 HIS PRETEND FIANCÉE—Victoria Pade
Manhattan Multiples
Josie Tate was the key to getting firefighter Michael Dunnigan's matchmaking mother off his back. Josie needed a place to stay—and Michael offered his apartment, *if* she would help him make his family believe they were engaged. It seemed like a perfectly practical plan—until Josie's heart got involved….

#1565 THE BRIDE WORE BLUE JEANS—
Marie Ferrarella
Fiercely independent June Yearling was not looking for love. Her life on the farm was more than enough for her. At least before businessman Kevin Quintano walked into her life…
and unleashed a passion she never thought possible!

#1566 FOUR DAYS, FIVE NIGHTS—Christine Flynn
They were stranded in the freezing wilderness and pilot Nick Magruder had to concentrate on getting his passenger, veterinarian Melissa Porter, out alive. He had no time to dwell on her sweet vulnerability—or the softness and heat of her body—as he and Mel huddled together at night….

SSECNM0803